TO LOVE AT (

Jennifer Drewett is the author of *To Love At Comic Con*, her debut novella. A Cardiff-born, Bristol-raised woman, she is now based in Brighton. Working part time as a medical receptionist, she spends her free time looking for the next story to write. You can catch up with her on her writer's page: *www.facebook.com/JenniferDrewettWriter*

TO LOVE AT COMIC CON

Jennifer Drewett

FIRST EDITION

Chapter One

The sun beamed across the skies of
Wichama at two o'clock on a bright
afternoon. The end house of the secluded
cul-de-sac of Baker Close was particularly
quiet. The inside of the house was full of
cliche quotes about love and interspersed
with memorabilia from 'Super Ginge' and the
TV show 'The Explorer' on the walls.

Sean, a handsome man in his late
twenties, was concentrating on hand-sewing a
patch on a shirt. Whilst he was doing his best
to not make any mistakes, he was also trying
to be quick with his stitching. This caused
visible amounts of stress, but he pushed on,
keen to finish as soon as he could.

As he threaded the needle to tie off the last stitch, the bedroom door swung open violently. His girlfriend Alexia stormed through the room with an empty suitcase. She threw it on the sofa so close to Sean that it almost hit him. He was careful not to stab himself with his needle in spite of being shaken up by the suitcase. He turned to face Alexia.

"Careful! I'm sewing," Sean said as calmly as he could. He quickly turned away and made sure his sewing was finished. When he turned back, Alexia was gone. He looked over at the suitcase and was irritated to see that it was empty.

"Fuck" he muttered to himself. He folded the shirt he was working on and placed it in the suitcase. He started packing it with clothes when a message came up on his phone. He ignored it and kept packing until it started ringing.

Whilst the sun beamed on Wichama, it was nowhere to be seen in Cicestre. That didn't bother Polly, a tidy woman in her mid-twenties, as she was busy packing a suitcase. She folded her costume parts and placed them carefully into the suitcase, which was open on her bed. She was meticulous and calm about the organisation of her luggage. Her bedroom was a nerd heaven with prop weapons, posters and pictures from countless cons all over the wall. As she laid the final costume part into the suitcase, she received a message on her phone. She took one glance at it and sighed.

Fuck off, she thought to herself, *I'd have to be desperate to go back to that.* She opened the message only to delete it. Feeling a small wave of relief, Polly went into her drawer and found her make-up bag. She placed it neatly in her suitcase, then left the room to go into her bathroom. She methodically picked up her toothpaste, shampoo, toothbrush and deodorant and placed them into a washbag, before turning to a small, locked chest next to her sink. She crouched down, unlocked the chest, and retrieved a small, tied bag. She got up, and headed back into her bedroom. She placed both bags neatly into her suitcase and carefully closed it as her phone began to ring.

Meanwhile in a city called Mancunio, a family home housed an enthusiastic twenty-something nonbinary person called

Jamie. They came into their living room with a full suitcase and placed it carefully by their door. Without skipping a beat, they ran up the hallway stairs. A few moments passed before Jamie came barrelling down the stairs and back into the living room, this time with a full backpack. They placed it next to the suitcase, then sat down on their sofa in their living room, which was adorned with a variety of family photos and pottery.

They looked at their clock. It had just turned 2:30. They started to tap their lap in excitement. Unable to sit still, they grabbed their phone and began texting. As they texted, a broad smile etched across their face. They put their phone down next to them. They looked at the clock, looked back at their phone, looked back at the clock then looked back at their phone. They sighed in boredom.

"I'm so early," they thought, "I wonder if the others are ready." With that, they grabbed their phone. They went into the group chat with Polly and Sean and pressed the call button.

"Hello?" Polly calmly answered. Sean was less composed with his "Hey".

"Are you two ready yet?" Jamie enquired hopefully.

"Almost done Jamie," Polly laughed, "What about you, Sean?"

"Not even close, Polly. Alexia is doing *something* of some description while I pack."

"Does she even *know* how to pack?" Polly retorted sarcastically.

"It'll be fine once we get to Brigstowe. I'm so excited!" Jamie nearly shrieked down the phone.

"It'll be great to see everyone again. Are we all staying at The Plaza?" Polly asked.

"I know I am." Jamie answered.

"Yeah, same. Do we know where Danni and Reuben are staying?" Sean wondered.

"The Plaza. So are Mal & Leo." Polly responded.

"I would've thought Mal would be staying at The Grand? Isn't that where the con usually puts their paid workers?" Jamie asked as they distractedly fiddled with their hair.

"Usually, but considering what happened last time with whatshisname, the con booked him at The Plaza." Polly said.

"Can't believe the con booked him again after what he did to Leo."

"I suppose because Leo wasn't the one working for the con, they decided it wasn't their business."

"But he's the spouse of one of their employees. Surely that's not on..." Sean was unable to finish the train of thought thanks to an angry "SEAN!" shouted by Alexia from downstairs.

"Are you done packing yet?" Sean sighed.

"Bollocks." He muttered to himself. He knew he had to get back to packing.

"I'm sorry. I've got to go. I'll see you at the hotel later?" Sean asked.

"Alright. I can't wait!" Jamie said with glee.

"Try not to have World War III beforehand, yeah?" Polly quipped to Sean. He laughed a little.

"No promises" Sean hung up and continued to pack.

It was 11pm at the Brigstowe Plaza. The night was calm and still with barely a soul to be heard, with the exception of the odd word spoken between a pair of smokers near the entrance. The almost-silence was broken by the sound of a rolling suitcase. Sean pulled a large suitcase on wheels whilst Alexia walked next to him carrying a smaller bag.

Despite the hour, the hotel foyer was a hub of activity in contrast to the outside as Sean and Alexia entered. One of the receptionists was on the phone, whilst their colleague tried to look busy - probably because a manager was walking by the desk making notes.

"Shall we check in?" Sean gestured to the desk.

"No I thought we should go home," Alexia sighed. "Don't be stupid, Sean." They headed for the front desk.

"Hi, we're here to check in," Sean said to the second receptionist.

"Don't flirt with her, Sean. I'll deal with this." Alexia snapped. She turned to the receptionist as Sean shuffled uncomfortably.

A lift pinged. It opened its doors. Two men in their thirties holding hands, Leo and Mal, got out of the lift. They walked by and spotted Sean and Alexia, who did not see them.

Not wanting to distract the pair, Leo and Mal headed into the hotel bar. It was notably quiet with a trio of friends at the bar talking to each other and sharing a bottle of wine. Leo and Mal looked around the bar and spotted Polly sitting alone reading a book.

"Polly!" Leo called. Polly looked up from her book.

"Leo and Mal. My favourite Knights." She smiled as they approached her. She stood up and hugged them both. They sat together.

"How're you two?" she asked.

"Great," Mal replied.

"We just witnessed the arrival of Mr & Mrs Hetero Dysfunction." Leo told Polly. She laughed. It wasn't the first time the pair had been described that way.

"Anything broken yet?" she pondered.

"They were subdued but it's only a matter of time," Mal answered, "I'll be shocked if it doesn't go south during Comic Con tomorrow."

"I don't know," Leo interjected, "Jamie told me that Sean got dragged into doing a couples' cosplay so maybe they'll be quietly tense."

"Shit! Which couple?" Polly asked with a small grin on her face.

"No idea," Leo replied , "but I can't wait to find out."

" Me neither," Polly giggled.

"Weren't you going to bring that guy with you this weekend - Don something?" Mal asked innocently.

"Nah," Polly quickly responded. "He was more into satisfying his car than satisfying me sexually. There's only so much a pretty face can compensate for."

"Better off without, then?" Leo said.

"Quite right," Polly agreed, "I'm a little tired. I'm going to have a bit of 'me' time."

"Okay. Tomorrow I'll be buried in cosplay competition prep," Mal said.

"I'll be around though," Leo piped up. "Want to head into con together?"

"Yeah, that'll be great," Polly replied. "See you at breakfast?"

"Yeah." Leo responded.

"Goodnight Pol," Mal said as he stood up. Leo and Polly also stood up.

"Night," Polly said as she grabbed her book, and headed for the lifts.

Chapter Two

Dawn was more than a few hours ago, but still the birds chirped their morning song for the late risers.

It was half past eleven, and several costumed people were leaving the hotel - not exactly in a convoy, but certainly all heading in the same direction.

Waiting by the hotel door and watching them leave, Polly checked herself out in the glass reflection. The coloured stripes down the front of the corseted dress stood out in the sunlight against the white fabric.

"Viola!" Leo exclaimed, wearing a t-shirt with a terrible nerdy pun. Polly rolled her eyes at him.

"Don't flip my car!" he said, in reaction to the eye-roll, "it's just had its MOT"

"Thanks." Polly giggled appreciatively.

"Are you competing?" Leo asked.

"In this Viola costume? No," she hesitated for a second, "I'm going to watch the competition though." At that moment, Jamie appeared between Leo and Polly.

"Are we ready to go?" Looking between themselves, Polly and Leo could see the style, the suit, the half unbuttoned shirt, and emphatic enthusiasm.

"Oh Explorer, what made you so excited?" Leo asked.

"Their beloved, Michael York is having an informal question and answer session at the event," Polly responded.

"It's less than 90 minutes away," Jamie said, with a hint of desperation.

"Leo, shall we walk the excited puppy to Comic Con?" Polly asked.

"The path has already been well trod." Leo gestured at the various groups who had already departed. Polly strode confidently, Leo casually sauntered, Jamie moved in as restrained and suave a manner as they could manage given their excitement.

The Brigstowe Convention Hall had a sparse, but growing, collection of people outside. Some were in groups chatting , while others posed for photos. The general mood was of relaxed happiness.

Inside the building was a different story. It was buzzing with activity. Among the stalls selling everything a geek could dream of, the costumed and uncostumed alike looked over the wares. Carpenters, crafters, and forgers were in their own dedicated Artist's Alley which, while a touch quieter, still hummed with interest and the exchanging of coin, both electronic and metal. There was a closed-off stage area being worked on by a team of people preparing for something big happening later. Some of the guests were answering questions on the small stage, while others were meeting fans, signing autographs, and complimenting especially fine homages to their work.

As they entered, the trio took in as much of the activity as they could see.

"How long have we got?" Polly asked Jamie.

"About an hour or so," they answered, "But I want to get there earlier to grab some good seats."

"Let's have a look around for a bit first," Leo suggested.

"Sounds good," Polly agreed. All three huddled together and started exploring the vast Comic Con before them.

Sean and Alexia were dressed as Super Ginge and Heidi Gertrude Duff from *Super Ginge*. Sean was wearing a ginger wig, a spandex style suit with a dance belt, and a cape. Alexia was wearing a very ordinary looking outfit with a t-shirt that said "I lie tangent to his curves" with a mathematical graph, fake glasses and a blonde wig. They were exploring the stalls together in silence.

"Shall we try and find some people?" Sean asked.

"You want to be away from me *that* much?!" Alexia snapped.

"No. I just wanted to see our friends." Sean responded meekly. Alexia huffed. Sean started looking around, searching for someone familiar to break the awkward tension. He wasn't successful and turned his attention back to Alexia right until he heard a familiar voice.

"Oi! Ginge!" Sean turned around to see who shouted at him. It was his friend Danni who waved at him. She was dressed as a zombified character from *Zombie Shield*. Seeing Danni made Sean's heart skip a beat for a brief moment. Just seeing her face made him feel instantly better. Pushing Danni's wheelchair was her boyfriend Reuben. He was dressed as a character named Enigma from *Zombie Shield*. He was half zombie, half human with half of his clothes in tatters and the other half looking pristine. Danni and Reuben approached Sean and Alexia but were met part way by Sean.

"That's *Super* Ginge to you," Sean joked with Danni as he hugged her. Alexia spotted this and made her way over, irritated that she had been left behind.

"I've missed you," Sean said as he went to shake Reuben's hand, maintaining eye contact with Danni.

"Missed you too, you soppy git." Danni responded with a smile. Reuben and Sean shook hands but Alexia clung on to

Sean's arm with force. This didn't go unnoticed by Reuben and Danni. The atmosphere immediately became tense.

"I see we have a little meeting going on," Alexia commented snidely.

"Hey Alexia," Danni greeted. "How're things?"

"Fine," Alexia responded coldly. Danni and Reuben looked at each other awkwardly. Reuben went back to stand behind Danni's wheelchair. The atmosphere was even more awkward, but Danni tried to ease the tension.

"Interesting costume choices. Have you seen Season 2 yet?" Danni enquired, keen to ease the tension.

"Well," Sean started.

"*He* hasn't but I have," Alexia interrupted with delight, "I just *love* the show."

"Jane has just started watching Season 1." Reuben joined in.

"Who?" Alexia asked rudely.

"My girlfriend?" Reuben answered, confused.

"Danni is your girlfriend." Alexia pointed out.

"So is Jane." Reuben responded, a little irritated. Danni looked at Sean who shrugged in confusion .

"Reuben and I are polyamorous, Alexia. Jane's a partner of his. I thought we already told you." Danni explained.

"I'm sure you did," Sean chimed in. "Maybe Alexia forgot."

"I didn't *forget*," Alexia interjected, "I just don't get it." There was an awkward silence as Reuben and Danni tried their best to process what just happened.

"Well then." Reuben blurted out. At that moment Jamie, Leo and Polly arrived. Jamie, still in an excitable mood, put their arms around Sean and Alexia. Danni and Reuben were visibly relieved to see more of their friends arrive.

"Hello all," Jamie squealed.

"We've brought a puppy with us," Polly joked. She hugged Danni.

"Good timing?" Polly whispered to Danni.

"The best." Danni whispered back as Polly broke away from her.

"Michael York's Q&A is due to start in 45 minutes. Anyone want to come get seats with me?" Jamie asked the group.

"Alexia, didn't you want to get into cosplaying from The Explorer? That's Michael's niche." Polly suggested.

"Oh perfect, you can come," Jamie proclaimed as they linked arms with a reluctant Alexia. Alexia and Jamie started to leave.

"What about -?" Alexia started.
" They'll catch up later. Come on! It's *Michael York*!" Jamie interrupted as they left with her. Sean, Danni and Reuben breathed audible sighs of relief. Polly broke out into laughter.

"Holding up there, Pol?" Leo asked, amused.

"Fucking hell Sean," Polly gasped through laughter, "You don't even *like Super Ginge*."

"I know," Sean said, defeated.

"What possessed you to go along with it?" Leo asked, perplexed.

"I really can't remember." Sean responded with some sadness in his voice.

"Whatever happened, you're among friends now." Danni chimed in reassuringly. Sean looked at Danni and smiled at her. She smiled back.

"Have you been able to check out the con properly?" Reuben asked the group.

"A little," Leo replied.

"Are any of you competing at the contest today?" Sean inquired.

"I am!" Reuben happily answered, "I've got to grab some food before I go to pre-judging."

"Why don't you go and do that now? The rest of us can go round the con and make sure we've got seats for the cosplay contest." Polly suggested.

"Super Sean can push Danni's chair," Leo proposed.

"If that's okay with Sean?" Danni checked, not wishing to impose on her friend.

"No problem," Sean said in a jokey hero voice, "for no task is too much for Super Ginge!"

"Thanks man," Reuben said to Sean. Reuben kissed Danni on the lips.

"I'll see you after the contest," he said, "I love you."

"I love you too. You'll be amazing out there." Danni told him. Reuben smiled at Danni. He turned to Polly, Leo and Sean.

"I'll see you all later." Reuben left. Sean moved behind Danni and grabbed the handles of her wheelchair.
"Where shall I take you, Zombie Ma'am?" Sean said in his joke hero voice. Danni laughed. Polly and Leo couldn't help but notice.

"Artists Alley, everyone? I haven't been yet." Danni proposed.

"Sounds good," Polly agreed.

"Let's go!" Leo pointed to Artist Alley as he led the group away.

45 minutes ticked by. Alexia and Jamie sat in the now-full seating area of the

smaller stage, waiting for Michael York to start his Q&A. Alexia looked around.

"Where the hell is Sean?" she barked.

"I'm sure he'll be on his way," Jamie lied.

"We were meant to spend this Comic Con time *together*, not apart. Why is he avoiding me?" Alexia complained.

"Don't you live with each other?" Jamie sniped back. They instantly regretted saying that. Alexia was about to answer when an announcer stepped onto the stage.

"Folks, thank you all for coming to this Q&A. Without further delay, here's Michael York!" The announcer declared to the crowd, who thundered into cheers and applause. Michael, a strikingly handsome man in his thirties, strutted on to the stage dressed as *The Explorer* in an outfit similar to Jamie's. Jamie cheered whilst Alexia calmly clapped, seething on the inside. Jamie was visibly excited.

"He's beautiful!" Jamie squeaked. Michael shook hands with the announcer and sat.

"Thank you. Hello Brigstowe!" Michael said to the crowd who cheered back.

"You've been a great audience already," Michael joked.

"I've got a few questions to ask you then I'll open the floor to the audience to ask questions." The announcer told Michael. Jamie smiled. Alexia looked around the stage area entrance to see if Sean was there. When she didn't see him, she turned her attention back to the stage.

Chapter Three

45 more minutes went by. Polly, Leo,
Sean and Danni were wandering around
Artists Alley. They were taking in all the
amazing art and comic work available. Danni
and Sean were lost in conversation with each
other, browsing the right-hand side of the
alley. Polly and Leo decided to look around
the tables on the left-hand side. They
encountered a table full of Sara-Fi comics and
prints. Polly was immediately drawn to the
art.

"Nice Viola cosplay," a voice
complimented Polly. Polly looked up from
the art to see the person who complimented
her. Mara, a trans woman in her mid-thirties,
was dressed mostly in black. Polly looked at
her. She knew who she was, but it was as if

she was looking at her for the first time. She lost herself as she felt an instant attraction to Mara. She is uncharacteristically unsure of what to say. Mara smiled at her. Leo listened into their interaction.

"Thanks. I put it together myself." Polly answered Mara. She instantly regretted it, feeling as if she sounded a bit obvious.

"It's lovely." Mara further complimented her. Leo smirked as he continued to pretend to look at the artwork.

"I'm -" Mara started.

"Mara Helinski," Polly interrupted out of nerves, "I know. I've read your Sara-Fi comics."

"Oh, you have?"

"Yeah. My friends and I really enjoy them."

"I'm glad to hear that." There was a pause.
Leo looked up.

"Have you finished writing the
Nymeria arc? I'm on tenterhooks for the next
issue." Leo asked.

"Yeah, at last! It won't be long till I
send it off to the publishers." Mara answered.
Leo smiled. He looked at Polly who was
fidgeting with her costume, not sure what to
say or do. What she was feeling was entirely
new to her. At that moment, Sean and Danni
appeared. Danni was immediately taken by
the Sara-Fi artwork.

"Oh, this is amazing." Danni
remarked.

"Thanks!" Mara replied.

"I hate to rush off on one of my
favourite comic writers, but we've got to
head to the cosplay competition," Danni

explained, "I want to make sure I can get a decent aisle position."

"They've got a designated area for folks with mobility aids towards the front this time. Let's head over!" Leo told Danni. Danni, Sean and Leo started to leave. Polly joined them.

"Hey! Viola!" Mara shouted out to Polly. Polly stopped. She faced Mara.

"I never caught your actual name." Mara pointed out.

"I'm Polly," Polly replied as she smiled, "Polly Guilder." Leo, Danni and Sean stopped as they realised Polly wasn't with them. They turned to see her with Mara.

"Well Polly Guilder, want to go for a drink later?" Mara asked. Polly was a little taken aback.

"Sure. I'd like that." She accepted without hesitation.

"I'm staying at The Plaza. I can meet you at the bar. 8 okay?" Mara suggested.

"I'll be there." Polly agreed. Polly and Mara smiled at each other. The obvious sexual tension between the two didn't go unnoticed by Sean, Danni and Leo. Polly waved goodbye to Mara, turned and went straight to her friends. Leo was about to say something.

"Wait." Polly stopped him.

At the same time, Alexia and Jamie were still at Michael York's Q&A. Michael was being interviewed by the announcer on stage. Jamie was watching every moment with keen attention whilst Alexia was grumpy at Sean's absence.

"For the last 15 minutes, I'm going to get members of the audience to ask you questions, Michael." The announcer told the excited audience, "Hands up if you want to ask and one of the helpers will come to you with a microphone. Who'd like to go first?" A rush of people, including Jamie, put their hands up. Alexia was a little bemused by this.

"I thought you knew everything there is to know about this man?" Alexia asked, somewhat jaded.

"You can never know too much about someone, am I right?" Jamie retorted happily. Before Alexia could respond, a helper handed a microphone to Jamie. They stood up and faced Michael who had his attention on them. Their heart was in their mouth as they spoke.

"Hi" Jamie said into the microphone.

"Great costume choice. You've put it together well." Michael complimented Jamie. They blushed as a round of applause rung out. Michael gave Jamie a dazzling smile which made them want to swoon into his arms.

"Thank you." Jamie paused. "I wanted to ask: What do you enjoy most about judging cosplay competitions?" The audience turned their attention to Michael. He kept his attention on Jamie.

"That's a good question. I enjoy seeing the creativity and skill that go into the costumes. What I love even more is the courage of the competitors to go on stage in front of an audience of strangers. Just getting out there makes you a winner regardless." Michael answered honestly. Jamie was enthralled with Michael as another charming smile crossed his face.

"Thank you." Jamie handed the microphone back to the helper and sat back down. The Q&A continued as Jamie turned to face Alexia, star struck and incredibly happy.

"He's wonderful." Jamie squeaked quietly.

"He is quite a dish." Alexia agreed.

"He's so dreamy. He must be an incredible boyfriend."

"He's probably swamped by women."

"I want him to swamp *me*." Alexia was somewhat perplexed by what Jamie just said. She tried to think of a response but came up short.

"He's judging the cosplay competition today. I want to watch." Jamie continued.

"We need to find Sean first." Alexia pointed out.

"He'll probably be watching it with the others."

"Does he have to watch it without me?"

"Why don't we head to the cosplay stage area and get seats? That way you can watch it together."

"Good." Jamie and Alexia got up and started to leave.

Fifteen minutes elapsed . On the cosplay stage area, Mal was doing some vocal exercises. There were several people sitting in the stage seats in groups. Danni, Sean, Polly and Leo came in. Mal spotted them and immediately came to them. He kissed Leo.

"How's your day been?" Mal asked.

"It's been fairly good." Leo responded.

"Yeah the con is quite fun." Polly affirmed.

"Are you sure you mean the con or tonight's date?" Leo joked.

"Bugger off, Leo." Polly said, annoyed.

"It was adorable." Danni remarked.

"I'm shocked you noticed, Danni. You and Sean seemed quite pre-occupied," Leo jabbed.

"I think I got carried away with human interaction that didn't involve pouting or sulking." Sean pointed out.

"Speaking of pouting," Mal interjected, "I think you folks need to get some seats. It'll start to fill up in a minute."

"I hear you have a proper disabled-friendly viewing area." Danni inquired.

"Yep but you can only have one person with you. I assume Mr Ginge will be your companion?" Mal explained.

"Is that okay with everyone else?" Danni asked the group.

"You go on ahead. We'll try and keep seats for Jamie and Alexia so they're with us." Polly answered.

"Shit, won't Alexia be annoyed she's not with you?" Danni asked Sean.

"She might," Sean said coolly, "But I've had too good a day to care." Danni and Sean smiled at each other, something that didn't go unnoticed by the rest of the group.

"Right," Mal said to Danni and Sean, "Come with me then." He escorted Danni and

Sean to the disabled viewing area. Polly and Leo found four seats and put their coats on two to save them for Jamie and Alexia.

"Is it wrong that I want those two crazy kids to get together?" Leo asked Polly.

"A little." She answered, "I don't think they realise what's going on between them. I'm worried Danni will get hurt."

"Because of Alexia?"

"Because of Sean."

"Sean?"

"He won't get his shit together. He's being damaged by his existing relationship. Dragging Danni into it isn't fair."

"That's surely for them to deal with if it happens."

"Of course. They're adults. It doesn't stop me from worrying." At that exact moment, Jamie came rushing over with an annoyed Alexia. She was looking around trying to find Sean.

"How was the Q&A?" Polly asked.

"Good." Alexia answered.

"Where were you guys?" Jamie enquired.

"We got a bit caught up with Polly's love life ." Leo teased.

"Juicy!" Jamie exclaimed, "I want to hear all about it."

"Where's Sean?" Alexia asked curtly.

"He's fine. He's with Danni in the disabled viewing section." Polly answered hesitantly.

"I should go with him then," Alexia was about to leave but Mal stepped in front of her.

"Hey, Alexia! Having a good day?" Mal asked politely.

"Is Sean in the disabled area?" Alexia responded, irritated.

"Yeah, he's with Danni," Mal answered.

"Well, I should go over there." Alexia stated. She tried to move but Mal stopped her.

"You can't. Danni is only allowed one person with her." Mal explained.

"Where's Reuben, then?" Alexia indignantly asked.

"He's competing today."

"Oh." An awkward pause fell. Jamie put their arm around Alexia.

"Don't worry," Jamie tried to assure her, "We'll keep you company." Leo grabbed the coats he used to reserve seats and Jamie and Alexia sat down.

Chapter Four

Half an hour went by. Reuben sat backstage of the cosplay area, twiddling his fingers in anticipation. His phone went off. It was a text from Danni that read: "Good luck. You'll smash it. I love you xxx". Reuben smiled. He was about to put his phone away when he got another text message. It was from Jane: "Good luck. I believe in you. Love you lots xxx" Reuben smiled even more and sighed in gratitude. He put his phone away.

Meanwhile, at the disabled seating area, Danni was putting her phone away after texting Reuben. The seats behind them were starting to fill up with people.

"Sending Reuben some last-minute luck?" Sean asked.

"Yeah. I feel I've kind of neglected him a bit today. I know Jane would be texting him too but that's no reason to slack off in the girlfriend department." Danni answered.

"You had fun today?"

"Of course. It was really good to hang out with you."

"Same. I haven't had that much fun at comic con in a long time." Danni and Sean kept looking at each other, smiling. A clear sexual and romantic tension between the two of them that went beyond a platonic relationship was very much present.

The moment was broken when Sean received a text from Alexia: "Come back to me. You've spent enough time with her." Sean instantly deflated. Danni noticed.

"What's wrong?" Danni asked. Sean shook his head, not wanting to answer. Danni held his hand. He faced her. His eyes met hers. In a look Danni could tell what was going on. She squeezed Sean's hand and smiled. He returned with a little smile and held her hand back. At that moment, the lights dimmed. Sean and Danni turned away from each other to face the stage. Danni went to her phone. At that the stage lights went on. Mal strode confidently on stage as a round of applause greeted him.

"Hello Brigstowe Comic Con. Have you all had a good day?" Mal asked enthusiastically. The crowd cheered.

"Are you ready to watch the competition cosplayers?" Mal grinned. The crowd cheered again.

"Good! That's what we like to hear. Before we meet our cosplayers, let's go through some housekeeping rules." Whilst

Mal continued to speak on stage, Polly received a text from Danni: "Please find a way to stop Alexia texting Sean? She's upsetting him. Drink on me later xxx". Polly spotted Alexia clutching her phone next to Leo. Polly, now realising what was going on, tapped Leo on the shoulder. She showed him the text from Danni. He read it, turned to Alexia and tapped her on the shoulder. She turned to face him. At that moment Polly leant over Leo and snatched Alexia's phone from her. Alexia tried to protest but Polly gestured at her to be quiet.

"Either you stay and watch the contest, or you fuck right off." Polly whispered angrily. Alexia, sensing she was outnumbered, backed off and looked to the stage. Mal had now finished discussing the housekeeping rules.

"Now the boring bit is done, let's welcome the judges!" Mal announced. With that, Michael and two other cosplayers emerged onto the stage, waving at the audience who clapped and cheered. Jamie clapped and cheered particularly enthusiastically which didn't escape Leo and Polly's attention.

"These lovely folks will have the unenviable task of judging our contestants today. They shall now take their seats." Michel and the other judges went to their seats, close to the disabled viewing area.

"Lucky Danni & Sean! They're so close to Michael" Jamie whispered. Leo giggled. Mal took centre stage again.

"The first three contestants on stage today will be competing for a place in The Creator Channel's National Cosplay

Championship at the end of the year and a £500 prize." The crowd whooped.

"First contestant today is Jolz 2 Holz Cosplay as Nurse Zelda from 'Nurse Limbo'!" Mal left the stage. Jolz 2 Holz Cosplay came out in her Nurse Zelda costume to a rowdy round of applause. For her performance she lip synced to some dialogue followed by singing the theme tune. At the end of her performance, she bowed. The crowd cheered and clapped as she left the stage. Mal came back on stage.

"Next contestant is Lil Royale as The Explorer from The Explorer!" Mal left the stage as Lil Royale strode confidently onto the stage to an enthusiastic round of applause. They performed a monologue from the show. Once they were done, they left the stage thanking the audience as they went. Mal reappeared again .

"The final competitive contestant is Reuben Cosplay as 'Enigma' from Zombie Shield!" Mal announced. He left the stage as Reuben appeared. Sean, Polly, Leo, Jamie, Danni & Sean cheered extra loudly for him along with everyone else cheering him on. Reuben rocked the stage with a comedy stand-up routine based on his character's dating exploits. Every joke got increasing amounts of laughter from the audience. As he finished, he got a lot of cheers and applause especially from his friends and partner. As he left the stage he spotted Danni and winked at her. Danni's smile widened.

Some time passed. The competition was over, and the audience were leaving the stage area. Outside Polly, Leo, Alexia and Jamie were standing about waiting.

"Why isn't Sean here yet?" Alexia complained.

"He has to push Danni's chair through the crowds." Leo pointed out. Alexia pouted. Leo, Polly and Jamie chose to ignore her. At that moment Reuben arrived with his certificate, trophy and prize envelope. He was grinning from ear to ear.

"All hail our noble champion!" Polly exclaimed jokingly. Jamie, Leo and Polly bowed to him. Alexia watched but didn't join in. Mal walked up to the group.

"My noble subjects, your Master is weary but accepts your gracious greetings. He seeks Lady Daniella and Sir Sean." Reuben said in a fake noble voice.

"Noble champion," Mal joined in, "I believe the Lady and Sir you seek are sailing the Sea of the Slow Crowd Movers."

"Their journey may be arduous," Reuben continued, "But their hearts are strong. They shall venture forth and not stop until they reach their destination." It was then that Sean and Danni came up to the group. Alexia started staring daggers at Sean, who rushed Danni to Reuben.

"My Lady Daniella!" Reuben proclaimed as he bent down on one knee to Danni, "I have returned with treasure!"

"Sir Reuben, you're a dork but I'm very proud of you." Danni giggled. Reuben kissed her and they embraced briefly. Sean moved away from behind Danni's chair. Reuben gave Danni the trophy, envelope and certificate to hold on to. He stood where Sean had been. Sean was now standing next to Alexia, who could barely contain her annoyance. She put her arm around Sean's arm with a vice-like grip.

"Alright folks," Reuben turned to face the rest of the group, "What's the plan for tonight?"

"Dinner and drinks at Sorrow No More pub?" Mal suggested.

"Sounds good to me," Danni agreed, "Shall we say 8pm? That'll give us enough time to de-cosplay and get into civilian clothes."

"I think we all know where Polly will be." Leo teased.

"Leo!" Polly reacted, slightly exasperated.

"Alright." Leo backed down.

"Sean, I trust we'll see you and Alexia there?" Jamie asked Sean.

"Yeah -" Sean started.

"Actually, we'll be seeing Sean's sister Ariana." Alexia interrupted.

"Oh, Ariana would be more than welcome to join us!" Jamie insisted.

"We'd probably end up at Sorrow No More anyway so we may as well be all together." Sean explained.

"I thought you wanted to spend proper time with your sister." Alexia pouted.

"I can socialise with more than one person at a time." Sean argued. Alexia huffed. The situation was awkward.

"If Ariana is alright with it, you're welcome to join us," Mal chipped in.

"We'll let you know." Sean said.

"Shall we all get sorted?" Reuben proposed. With that, Alexia took Sean with her and rushed to leave with him following reluctantly.

"I'm almost sorry to miss the carnage tonight," quipped Polly.

"Is she always that pissy?" Leo quizzed.

"I swear they were lovey dovey at *some* point." Danni insisted.

"Since when?" Reuben challenged.

"A long time ago?" Danni hesitantly answered.

"I'm far too tired to deal with this nonsense right now. Shall we just head back to the Plaza?" Mal suggested.

"Good idea. Polly can fill me in on this date she's got." Jamie keenly said. Leo

and Mal started to leave; followed closely by
Danni, Reuben, Jamie and Polly.

Chapter Five

7:30pm rolled around. Polly was
sitting on her double bed at The Brigstowe
Plaza. She was in her pyjamas, staring at two
dresses laid out in front of her and trying to
decide which one to wear. A knock sounded
on her door. She rushed to open it. Jamie
came through. Their hair was styled nicely,
and they were wearing a freshly ironed shirt
with formal jeans.

"Interesting date outfit." Jamie
remarked. Polly ignored their comment. She
grabbed the dresses and showed them to
Jamie.

"What's a better look: accidental butt
exposure or tits out for all?" Polly asked
Jamie. Jamie thought for a minute.

"My queer non-binary senses are drawn to tits out for all." Jamie concluded.

"Thanks" Polly thanked as she threw the 'accidental butt exposure' dress by her suitcase. She headed into the bathroom to get dressed. Jamie sat on the bed.

"You're going to be fine." Jamie reassured her .

"I've never been on a date with a woman before." Polly fretted.

"Never too late to give it a go." Jamie joked.

"I'm straight though. Or at least I'm sure I am."

"You can't control who you're attracted to. It sounds like you're rather taken with Mara."

"What makes you say that?"

"You've never needed any of us to help you pick out an outfit for a date before." Polly opened the door. She was now dressed. She went to the dressing table where her make-up was laid out and started putting on her mascara.

"Whatever happens, you know it won't change how much we love you. With exception to Alexia and Sean, we're all already riding the queer train." Jamie consoled. Polly shot Jamie a small smile. She continued to put her make-up on.

"So, what are you all dressed up for?" Polly asked.

"Damn. I was hoping you wouldn't notice." Jamie cursed.

"Unexpected dates don't hamper my powers of deduction, Jamie."

"I may have been a little obvious with this outfit."

"You want to look good in case you run into Michael."

"I - I mean it can't hurt to look good at all times."

"No. Just don't get your hopes up super high."

"I won't. That way if I don't see him, I can't be disappointed. If I do, then it'll be the start of our perfect romance."

"You're an incurable optimist."

"You know it."

It was 8pm. Mal and Leo were sitting at a table at the Sorrow No More pub with 5 empty chairs. Mal leant on Leo's shoulder. Leo kissed him on the head. They both looked a little too tired to be out. They had glasses of soda in front of them.

"If none of the heteros show up, shall we have a movie and snuggle evening?" Leo asked.

"I would point out the inaccuracies of calling all of them heteroes, but I am too mentally tired to care." Mal sighed.

"Okay, the heteroes and Danni."

"And Jamie."

"And Jamie."

"And Reuben."

"Wait - Reuben too?"

"He is the straightest presenting bisexual man ever." Jamie responded as they stood in front of Leo & Mal with a pint of beer in their hand. They put the pint of beer down.

"Sorry I'm late. I was seeing Ms Guilder off on her date," Jamie explained as they took a seat next to Leo.

"How was she?" Leo inquired.

"Pretty nervous in a very Polly way." Jamie answered.

"Has she ever been on a date with a woman before?" Mal quizzed.

"No, but like I said to her, it's never too late to start." Jamie responded. They started looking around the room. They were searching for Michael but didn't see him anywhere. Mal noticed Jamie's distracted look.

"The others aren't here yet." Mal told them.

"Yeah. Who else is joining us?" Jamie asked.

"Danni & Reuben are on route. Sean said he, Alexia and his sister will come too but you know what they're like." Leo returned. Sean and Alexia arrived, accompanied by Ariana, Sean's stylish older sister.

"Hey guys." Sean said. Jamie turned around. They stood to face Ariana.

"It's good to see you again, Ariana." Jamie greeted.

"You too Jamie!" Ariana smiled as she hugged Jamie. Alexia took Sean by the hand to get seats. Ariana sat down next to Alexia. Jamie returned to their seat next to Sean and Leo.

"I'm Mal. This is my husband Leo." Mal introduced himself.

"Lovely to meet you." Ariana responded.

"So, Ariana: did you bring any baby Sean pictures?" Leo asked cheekily.

"Damn," Ariana chuckled. "Maybe next time. How was the comic con?"

"Pretty great," Jamie answered.

"You spent most of it gawping at Michael York." Sean retorted.

"You say that like it's a bad thing. Would you rather I gawp at you instead?" Jamie flirted slightly. Sean was about to answer when Alexia put her hand on Sean's as if to stop him,

"Baby, why don't you get us some drinks?" Alexia suggested. She raised her eyebrows at Sean. He stood up. He was about to leave to go to the bar when Danni and Reuben showed up. Danni was now using a walking stick to move with. Sean was taken aback for a moment by Danni's appearance.

Despite knowing her for so long, it was almost as if he was looking at her for the very first time. Alexia was visibly displeased but tried her best to cover it. She didn't fully notice Sean's reaction; however, Ariana noticed.

"Hey" Sean greeted Danni & Reuben. With that, Jamie turned to see them. They immediately stood up to face them.

"I just realised we're down a chair. Why don't you both take a seat and I'll find another one?" Jamie offered. Before anyone could react. Jamie left to find another chair. Danni took the chair Jamie was sitting on. Reuben placed his jacket on a seat next to Ariana and headed to the bar with Sean. They stood next to each other. It was quite busy at the bar as they waited to be served.

"Busy tonight." Sean commented.

"Well, it is a Saturday on comic con weekend," Reuben responded, "I can't be surprised." There was a moment of silence between them before Reuben faced Sean.

"Hey thanks for wheeling Danni and hanging out with her today. She had a great time."

"She's a complete joy to be around," Sean admitted with a smile. Reuben noticed. He looked around to make sure no one else could hear him.

"Do you fancy my girlfriend?" Reuben asked bluntly. Sean started to blush pretty hard. Reuben smiled.

"It's okay if you do. Just don't hurt her, yeah? I'd have to hurt you if you did." Reuben warned. At that moment, the bartender approached them. As Reuben ordered his and Danni's drinks, Sean was lost in thought, wondering where his feelings really lay.

Meanwhile, 8pm for Polly was vastly different than it was for her friends. She was all dressed up and visibly nervous. She went to the bar at The Plaza and waited to be served. The bar was quite quiet with murmurs of other conversations going on. Polly looked at her watch: it was 8:01pm. She sighed. "C'mon Guilder, don't be silly." She muttered to herself.. Whilst her attention was focused on the bar , Mara entered. She was dressed equally as wonderful as Polly. Mara spotted Polly and a small smirk crossed her face. She confidently headed over and stood next to Polly.

"Looks like I got here in time." Mara remarked. Polly turned to see her. She was taken aback with how she looked. For a moment, she was lost for words. She brought herself back with composure.

"I was about to order some drinks." Polly coolly replied.

"What's your poison?"

"Red Wine. Merlot."

"Excellent choice. Would I be presumptive in getting us a bottle?"

"Not at all. Are you sure you don't want me to pay half?"

"You can owe me for next time." Mara winked at Polly. She then turned her attention to the bartender who'd just come by. As Mara ordered, Polly was enthralled with her date. She barely realised when the wine arrived.

She snapped out of her reverie when Mara paid for the wine. The women walked from the bar to an empty table with their bottle of Merlot and two wine glasses. They set the items down on the table and took their seats. Mara opened the bottle of wine. She poured some into Polly's glass first. She looked into Polly's eyes.

"Say when," Mara asked as she poured the wine. Polly bit her lip slightly. She looked down at the glass which was slowly filling with wine. At a little over half full: "When." Polly instructed. Mara stopped pouring the wine into Polly's glass. She proceeded to pour wine into her own glass with about the same amount as Polly. She placed the wine bottle to one side. She picked up her glass and raised it to Polly.

"Cheers." Mara said. Polly raised her glass and clinked glasses with Mara.

"Cheers." Polly repeated. They both took a sip of their glasses.

"How did you find comic con today?" Polly asked Mara.

"Rather successful. The Nymeria arc has obviously been more successful than anticipated because that's almost all anyone asked about." Mara replied.

"That's a good thing, right?"

"Of course. I enjoy it when folks engage with my work."

"It's well earned."

"How was comic con for you?"

"Intriguing to say the least."

"Do tell." Mara raised her eyebrow. Polly took another sip of her wine . She put her glass down and looked at Mara.

"It's not really first date material." she admitted.

"That's fair. What would be 'first date' material?" Mara inquired. Polly paused for a moment.

"I work as a manager at a bookstore."

"That works. Do you enjoy it?"

"I enjoy books. Customers? Not so much."

"Isn't that the way in retail?"

"Maybe we should order some of your work for our store."

"Would you?"

"Yeah. That way I can see you more often, in a way." Polly felt slightly self-conscious after that remark and took a sip of her wine. Mara smirked and sipped her own.

"I'm sure there's a better way to see me more often." she replied. .

"You'd be up for that?" Polly asked.

"If the rest of the night is anything like this, then I wouldn't say no."

Chapter Six

A little later at the Sorrow No More pub, Reuben returned with his and Danni's drinks. He handed Danni her drink and gave her a peck on the cheek. Jamie returned with a chair and sat next to Reuben.

"So, Mr Champion, looking forward to the National Championships?" Mal asked Reuben.

"Of course. I get to subject thousands of people to my antics on tv. What's not to love?" Reuben replied joyfully.

"And that's why we love you." Leo smiled. Sean arrived with drinks for himself, Alexia and Ariana. He carefully placed the drinks on the table and sat down between Alexia and Danni.

"What was Michael like?" Jamie asked Reuben.

"He was pretty cool. He seems decent." Reuben nonchalantly answered.

"That sounds about right." Jamie sighed dreamily.

"Are you quite alright there, Jamie?" Danni asked .

"Excuse me while I fall in love a little more." Jamie replied.

"I managed to learn a bit more about cosplaying from 'The Explorer'. I just need to get Sean to cosplay him." Alexia chimed in happily.

"I haven't seen it in ages." Sean argued.

"I can get you up to speed." Alexia insisted. Sean wasn't interested but didn't want to say no either. This was clear to everyone else, and the atmosphere became tense.

"Reuben, what did you do for your performance today?" Ariana asked Reuben quickly. Reuben quite happily started telling her all about it whilst Jamie started a conversation about 'The Explorer' with Alexia. Leo and Mal started discussing the decor of the pub which left Danni and Sean to consider what drinks they wanted next.

It was a while into Mara and Polly's date at the Brigstowe Plaza hotel bar. Mara poured the last of the wine they had. They were both a little tipsy but nowhere near drunk.

"You haven't been on a date with a trans woman before, have you?" Mara blurted out. Polly was a bit taken aback by her observation .

"How can you tell?" Polly asked.

"You're confident but a bit unsure." Mara deduced.

"You're the first woman I've ever gone on a date with." Polly sighed.

"Oh."

"I never even considered the idea of dating another woman until we met."

"How're you finding it?"

"I'm having more fun than I usually do." Polly smiled. Mara smiled back at her and took a sip of her drink, finishing it.

"I don't get to date often. I think I just absorbed myself into my work. I could do with letting go a little." The sexual tension between the two women was distinct and present in the air. Polly was a little turned on as she finished her drink.

"Should we get another drink?" Polly asked.

"Perhaps... but maybe we should have it in my room." Mara suggested flirtatiously.

"That could work." Polly smiled.

Mara and Polly stood up, linked arms and walked out of the bar. They headed up in the lift, holding hands, until they got to the second floor. Polly felt exhilarated as it hit her what was going to happen. They reached Mara's hotel room. Mara got the hotel room door open, and they both entered. Mara shut the door behind her. She cupped Polly's face in her hand and stared into her eyes.. Mara kissed Polly gently. Their kiss turned passionate. Mara placed her hand down Polly's dress. A moment later, Polly started to moan as Mara played with her. Polly found the bottom of Mara's dress and starts to masturbate her as well. They were both incredibly aroused as they played with each other. They both came close to orgasm but then Mara gently moved Polly away from her. Polly laid on her front at the end of the bed. Mara started to have sex with Polly from behind. Polly clutched to the bed sheets as she became increasingly aroused. As the sex continued, Polly orgasmed in a way that she had never felt before. It was thrilling to feel so good in a way she never expected. Mara smiled and became more aroused as she felt Polly's orgasm. They continued to have sex until Mara orgasmed hard from behind. Polly panted, confused but satisfied at what just happened. As she started to stand up, Mara started to play with her clitoris to orgasm again. Afterwards, they both went to the bathroom to tidy themselves up. They held hands as they went back into the bedroom to talk some more. Polly felt both relaxed and conflicted at once. What did this mean? Did this mean anything for her?

Back at the Sorrow No More pub, Leo and Mal got up to leave. Everyone around them noticed.

"We're going to turn in." Mal told the table.

"You must be shattered." Danni remarked.

"It was good to meet you both." Ariana chimed in.

"Night folks." Leo said as he and Mal left. Alexia got up and faced Sean abruptly.

"We should think about going too."
Alexia announced to Sean.

"Oh? I was hoping to stay here a little
longer." Sean moaned. Alexia gave him an
annoyed look.

"Really?" Alexia demanded.

"You don't have to stay. You can go
back to the hotel room if you want." Sean
suggested. Alexia kept giving an annoyed
look. She turned to the others who'd fallen
awkwardly quiet.

"Fine. See you when you get to the
hotel." Alexia left in a huff. Sean let out a
sigh of relief when she was gone.

"What's up with you two?" Ariana
asked.

"We're having a bit of a rough patch.
She's just a bit overtired. It doesn't help that I

didn't spend the day with her." Sean explained, feeling deflated.

"*That's* a rough patch?" Reuben asked incredulously.

"Let's have another round and go back to having fun. Do we fancy a couple of cocktail pitchers?" Jamie quickly suggested.

"I can get behind that." Ariana replied.

"I'll come help." Reuben offered, and he and Jamie went to the bar together. Danni put her arm around Sean.

"You okay there?" Danni asked. Despite his numb mood, he felt a small thrill at Danni touching him even if only in a platonic way.

"More alcohol is the best way forward. Thanks." Sean answered. They smiled at each other. Danni moved her arm again.

"I'm going to go to the loo." Sean told the table as he got up and left for the toilets. Ariana sat next where Alexia was.

"You two are close?" Ariana asked.

"Always have been." Danni responded confidently.

"Be careful, Danni. I see the way you look at each other. If I didn't know better, I'd think there was something going on." Ariana warned. Danni was unsure how to respond. She fiddled with her walking stick.

"I don't mean to suggest you're doing anything wrong. You're being a friend and there's nothing wrong with that." Ariana softened, "I don't want either of you to get hurt. That's all."

"I appreciate that but there's nothing going on." Danni reassured her.

"I believe you." Ariana smiled at Danni.

"I'm pretty sure Alexia would have me murdered if anything *did* happen." Danni joked.

"I'd bet on you winning that scrap. Hypermobility is underrated." Ariana giggled.

"That and my walking stick is a mean hit." Danni laughed with Ariana. Sean came back and sat in between them.

"What's so funny?" Sean wondered.

"Nothing." Ariana winked at Danni. "You had to be there." At that, Reuben and Jamie returned with pitchers of cocktails in their hands.

"Let's get pissed!" Jamie shouted as everyone filled their glasses with drink. Jamie raised their glass.

"To friendship, comic cons and cheap cocktail pitchers!" Everyone clinked glasses and had a hearty drink. After they took a drink Jamie, Ariana and Reuben started talking to each other about Zombie Shield. Sean and Danni chanced a gaze at each other. Their romantic tension was clear. For a moment, it looked as if they might just kiss each other. This went unnoticed by the other three who were deep in conversation. Sean's phone went off with a text message alert: it was from Alexia demanding his return to the hotel. Sean was about to reply when his hand was held by Danni. His attention turned to her. She looked at him empathetically. It was a look Sean needed as he sighed deeply.

Danni smiled at him. He ignored his phone. They returned to the chat going on between their friends; however Danni couldn't help but feel a little confused by her own feelings and what just happened.

Chapter Seven

Two months flew by after the events
of Brigstowe Comic Con. The skies of
Brighthelmstone were patchy and cloudy,
which belied the summer sun that hid behind
the clouds. It was 6 o'clock in the evening. At
Danni & Reuben's flat, Danni was sitting at a
desk working on a costume. The bedroom
had a variety of posters on the wall with
blu-tacked photos from past comic cons on
one part. Danni was struggling to concentrate.
Her hands were starting to ache . She laid the
costume piece on her desk and placed her
hands on her lap to try and relieve the pain.
Reuben came into their bedroom wearing a
backpack with a glass of apple juice and a
straw in his hand.

"Don't work yourself too hard." Reuben warned her as he placed the apple juice on a coaster on the desk.

"Thanks," Danni said as she slowly moved her hands. "You off to Jane's?"

"Yeah. Will you be okay?"

"I'll be fine. I have my call in a moment. Go have fun."

"I love you."

"I love you too." Reuben kissed Danni and left, closing the door behind him. Danni started to sip on her apple juice when an alarm went off her phone. She looked at it.

"Ah! Perfect timing!" she thought as she grabbed her headphones. She went into her Messenger app, found a group conversation with herself, Sean, Jamie and Polly and pressed call. She propped her phone against her desk and wall.

At the same time in Cicestre, Polly was sitting in her bedroom. Dressed in a robe, she was brushing her hair looking quite bored. Don, still zipping up his jeans, came in looking quite pleased with himself. He ran his fingers through his hair.

"I knew you'd want me back." Don smirked. Polly put her hairbrush down, pissed at the remark.

"Don't flatter yourself," she responded curtly.

"Admit it: you can't resist me."

"Yes, I'm so horny for your ineffective dick and crap foreplay."

"You'll come crawling back for more."

"I doubt it now that I have AA batteries. Get out of my home." Not knowing how to respond, Don left. As soon as he went, Polly sighed. She looked at her phone resting on her table. She saw a message pop up from Mara. She turned her phone down. At that, her phone started to vibrate. She saw Danni calling.

"Oh shit, I forgot." she exclaimed as she connected her headphones to her phone.

Sean was trying to finish a work presentation on his laptop in Wichama. As he was trying to concentrate, he heard a cacophony of laughter from downstairs. He sighed, irritated. He looked at his laptop.

"Why couldn't they have drunk at one of *their* houses?" Sean muttered to himself. He continued to work on his presentation. Another clatter of laughter from downstairs once more ruined his concentration. He

closed his laptop lid in frustration. He looked
at his phone and went to his pictures. He
looked at pictures from Brigstowe Comic
Con and saw a group photo of himself, Polly,
Leo and Danni. He smiled as his thumb
caressed Danni's image. The fondness he felt
for the day he was remembering came
sweeping across his face. He felt the
happiness he felt being around his best friend.
Like nails to a chalkboard, the sound of
drunken laughter once again pierced through
Sean's reverie. He put his phone down.
Within seconds, it started to vibrate. He
smiled as he saw Danni calling.

"Thank fuck." he muttered as he
grabbed his earphones and plugged them into
his phone.

In Mancunio, Jamie was sitting in their bedroom: a small single bedroom with kids' space wallpaper. There were a number of memorabilia from 'The Explorer' adorning their wall. Jamie was browsing on their laptop looking at fabrics. As they lost themself in their browsing, their phone started to go off. It was Danni calling.

"Oh, it's call time!" Jamie exclaimed as they grabbed their headphones. They connected the headphones to the phone. They turned their camera on and saw Danni, Polly and Sean on the screen.

"Hi!" They all greeted each other with friendly affection.

"How are we all doing today?" Jamie innocently asked. The others collectively groaned.

"Who wants to go first?" Jamie laughed softly.

"My hands decided a pain flare up was in order." Danni complained.

"Are you okay?" Sean asked, concerned.

"I'll be alright. It happens. What's up with the rest of you?" Danni answered.

"I made the mistake of sleeping with Don." Polly admitted sheepishly.

"Don? I thought he was, and I quote, 'as useless as a flimsy dildo.'" Danni quipped.

"I did say it was a mistake." Polly defended herself.

"What happened to Mara?" Sean asked. Polly shuffled in place uncomfortably.

"I don't know. I find the whole thing confusing. I don't really want to talk about it." Polly quickly said as she suddenly stopped fidgeting.

"We won't push you Polly," Danni backed down, "What's up with you Sean?"

"Alexia decided to bring a bunch of her workmates over for pre-drinks before they go out." Sean moaned.

"How did you escape?" Polly enquired, cheekily.

"I told her I had a work presentation to do," Sean paused, "I actually *do* have one to do but I can't concentrate with this cackling going on."

"That sucks." Jamie sympathised, "In much happier news: at least we can cheer you up a bit by discussing Glyndŵr comic con. Are we all still going?"

"Of course. I managed to book the weekend off work without causing an international incident. I'm not skipping it for love nor money." Polly replied.

"Hell yeah. It'll be good to go back to the old stomping grounds," Danni responded wistfully.

"Do any of you need a hotel room buddy? I'm going to be coming on my own this time." Sean announced. Danni smiled a little, but she stopped herself from saying anything.

"How did you escape the Alexia jaws of death?" Polly wondered.

"She's away that weekend for a work training thing." Sean answered.

"She couldn't force you to come along?" Polly prodded further.

"Trust me: she tried." Sean sighed.

"Hey Danni, aren't you going alone?" Jamie chimed in. Danni began to blush slightly.

"Yeah. Reuben is going with Jane to see her family that weekend." Danni said hesitantly.

"Well, that solves that." Polly quickly decided.

"I'd be happy with it, and I know Reuben won't mind but won't Alexia have a fit?" Danni worried.

"She doesn't have to know, does she?" Jamie reasoned.

"Well -" Sean started.

"If you and Danni send me the money I'll book our rooms. At least when you say that I booked the room for you, you're not lying to her. Reuben is hardly going to tell Alexia anything else." Jamie interrupted.

"Reuben doesn't have her on social media." Danni pointed out.

"There! That's sorted. Now, are we all competing in the cosplay contest?" Jamie firmly changed the subject.

"Is a certain dreamboat of yours judging again?" Polly teased.

"Maybe?" Jamie coyly answered.

"I'm in if you are," Danni volunteered, "Maybe we can make these calls a regular thing to help encourage us?"

"Yay! Thanks Danni." Jamie thanked her. As the conversation continued Sean, Danni and Polly became more relaxed than they were.

Chapter Eight

A month elapsed. It was a cool Friday night. The clock outside struck midnight. The car park of the Glyndŵr hotel was packed full of cars. Polly came up to the hotel with a suitcase. She looked around as if she were looking for someone. Satisfied, she entered the hotel.

The Glyndŵr hotel foyer was noticeably quiet with barely a soul present. There was a single receptionist at the desk waiting for people to come. Polly came towards the reception desk.

"Hi, I'm checking in?" Polly told the receptionist.

"Certainly. What's the reservation name?" The receptionist asked.

"Ms Polly Guilder." Polly confirmed. As the receptionist looked for her reservation Polly saw Mara walk past from the bar area. Polly looked straight ahead and remained quiet as she waited for the receptionist. Mara walked past without acknowledging or seeming to notice Polly. Mara went up some stairs. Polly looked where Mara had gone. She felt weirdly hurt that she wasn't seen. She started to think back to the night at Brigstowe comic con.

"Okay ma'am I have seen your reservation. Here's your key," The receptionist said to Polly, snapping her out of her day dream. She handed her the key card.

"Thanks." Polly thanked her, still somewhat hazy.

"Breakfast starts at 7am and goes on until 11am each morning."

"Thanks." Polly grabbed her suitcase and headed to the hotel bar. The bar itself was relatively empty with the exception of a couple of lone men. She headed towards the bar until she heard:

"Polly!" Jamie shouted from across the room. Polly turned to see Jamie, Leo, Mal and Danni all with a glass of wine each. Jamie was finishing some sewing whilst Danni was reading a script and fiddling with her walking stick. Polly went over, grabbed a seat and let go of her suitcase. Danni put her script down and took a sip of her wine.

"Hello losers." Polly greeted everyone.

"We love you too, Guilder." Mal reproached.

"Was your journey okay?" Danni asked.

"It was alright. Where's Sean?" Polly enquired.

"He hasn't arrived yet." Danni confirmed sadly.

"I wonder what made him late *this* time." Leo sarcastically remarked.

"We'll have to see what excuse he comes out with." Polly joined in.

"Let's not be too hard on him folks," Danni cut in, "If Alexia has made him late, he probably doesn't need us to give him crap for it."

"I've texted him and told him where we are." Jamie told the group. With that, Sean came rushing through wearing a large backpack. His relief was palpable when he spotted the group sitting together.

"Thank fuck I'm here," Sean said as he reached the group.

"Well done for making it in one piece." Leo congratulated him.

"I hate to be antisocial, but I'm exhausted. I need to crash." Sean sighed.

"It is quite late," Danni agreed, "Why don't we all meet up at breakfast and head to con together?"

"I will have gone ahead of you all, but I'll probably see you during the cosplay competition." Mal told the group.

"Sing my praises to Michael for me?" Jamie jokingly asked.

"Nice try." Mal laughed. The group all stood up. Leo, Mal, Jamie and Danni finished their drinks.

"Can one of you help me up?" Danni asked the group.

"I will," Sean offered as he rushed over to her. A spark of romantic tension rose between the pair as they faced each other.

"Remember the elbows," Danni reminded him.

"Always." Sean affirmed. Sean held Danni's elbows as she held onto his. He hoisted her up and made sure she was steady before he let go of her. They were quite close to each other. The rest of the group watched without remark. Danni turned to get her walking stick.

"See you all at breakfast." said Polly.

The next morning dawned across the Glyndŵr skies. It was 9am. There were a few people in costumes hanging out outside the hotel. A couple of them headed inside with bags on them. The others seemed to be waiting around.

Inside the hotel, the restaurant had transformed into a continental breakfast bar. There was an extensive selection of breakfast options both hot and cold. On a table of five sat Danni in a very casual outfit of shirt and trousers. She sat with a full English breakfast, a cup of tea and some yoghurt. She was eating her breakfast when Polly came to the table with her cereal and a glass of juice. She sat opposite Danni.

"Hey" Danni greeted Polly.

"Hey you," Polly replied, "Did you sleep okay?"

"It was a bit spotty. My pain is being a bastard today."

"That sucks. How's Sean?"

"He seems okay. He was just getting changed when I came down. Come to think of it: he should've been down by now." Leo came into the breakfast room and joined Polly and Danni. He had a croissant, fresh fruit salad and a glass of water. He sat next to Polly. He was followed closely by Jamie who had a bowl of cereal and a cup of tea. They sat next to Danni. Both Leo and Jamie stared intently at Danni as they ate. Polly noticed.

"Folks, have you heard of the word 'subtle'?" Polly sarcastically asked.

"C'mon we're all thinking it." Jamie defended themself. Danni stared at them, annoyed.

"What?" she said, irritated. At that moment Michael walked past to get his breakfast. Jamie noticed. They stared at him without being noticed by him. Leo, Danni and Polly sighed.

"You've got it bad, mate." Leo remarked.

"He's so dreamy." Jamie sighed dreamily.

"Why don't you try talking to him?" Danni suggested.

"When I look like this? I'm going to sweep him off his feet when I look good. I've got to start on the right foot."

"You're just an eternal optimist, aren't you?" Polly declared.

"What?" Jamie squeaked.

"You're just so sure you can get with him. It's kind of admirable." Danni admitted.

"I've been dreaming of the perfect romance for forever. My dream person is nearly in my sights." Jamie explained.

"Be careful: I know he's a bit of a player," Leo warned Jamie. "Don't pin your hopes too high."

"You'll see, Leo," Jamie said defiantly, "I'll get him."

Danni finished eating. She looked at the time.

"Sean should've been ready by now." Danni moaned.

"Perhaps Alexia held him up?" Polly theorised.

"She's at a training course. How can she be holding him up?" Jamie asked.

"Text or call. I imagine a call." Leo answered.

"I'm going to get him some food. He'll miss breakfast at this rate." Danni decided.

"Shall we meet back at the entrance in an hour?" Polly suggested.

"That works," Leo agreed, "Danni, let me know if you need help getting Sean out. I will happily come and physically drag him down."

"I will," Danni responded, "See you all in an hour." She gulped down the rest of her breakfast and left to get more food.

Five minutes rolled by. Sean was stuck in his and Danni's hotel room on the phone to Alexia.

"Yeah look I really need to go and have some breakfast." Sean said down the phone.

"Are you trying to avoid me?" Alexia shrieked down the phone.

"What? No, I'm not trying to avoid you. I need to eat breakfast."

"You need to stay on the phone with me."

"I'm not staying on the phone whilst I eat."

"Why not?"

"I want to hang out with my friends."

"But I miss you."

"I know you miss me but -"

"Do you even care about me anymore?!"

"I do care!" Danni came through the door with food for Sean. He didn't notice her coming in. Danni placed her walking stick silently to the side.

"You can't expect me to stay on the phone 24/7. What if the venue has no signal? I won't be able to -" Sean began to explain.

"That's a pathetic excuse." Alexia interrupted.

"It's not an excuse. You know what convention halls are like."

"Well maybe you should do something about it."

"How am I meant to fix the lack of signal? Do you see how ridiculous you're being?" Alexia continued but Sean hung up. He sighed deeply as he sunk on to the bed. He looked up to see Danni holding breakfast for him.

"I figured you might miss breakfast, so I made sure you had some. Eat whilst I change." Danni told him, handing the food to Sean. She headed into the bathroom and shut the door. Sean sat up on the bed and ate his breakfast.

"What happened?" Danni asked from the bathroom.

"Alexia wants me to stay on the phone all day to her." Sean responded sadly.

"How was that supposed to work?"

"I have no fucking clue. She's going to blow up my phone all day and I'm not going to be able to enjoy myself."

"I've got an idea. Hold on."

Sean kept eating. A moment later, Danni came out of the bathroom wrapped in a towel but wearing tights. Sean stopped eating. Danni headed for her phone. She kept a hold of her towel. Sean could barely keep his eyes off of Danni, imagining what the towel was concealing. Danni fidgeted with her phone for a moment before putting it down. She headed back to the bathroom. Sean immediately turned his attention back to his breakfast.

"Check your phone." Danni shouted from the bathroom. Sean went to his phone. There were a number of message alerts from Alexia but there was a singular one from Danni. He opened the message. It was a screengrab of a phone screen with low signal and the time that read 11:32am.

"How did -?" Sean started.

"I figured this might happen, so I thought ahead. Now eat your breakfast and get changed. We have a comic con to enjoy." Danni interrupted. Sean smiled and continued eating his breakfast.

It was 10:30am. Polly was dressed as a vampiric character from a vampire horror called 'Lust at First Bite.' She was checking her messages but saw none. She did not notice Sean and Danni come by. Danni was in her wheelchair clutching her stick cosplaying Viola from 'Viola Love' whilst Sean was cosplaying as a Maître D from 'Cocktail Bar: The Musical.' He was pushing Danni's wheelchair. They spotted Polly and Sean was about to approach her, but Danni stopped him.

"I can use my telepathic mind powers to tell her we're here." Danni joked.

"I've got one better." Sean said as he went to Polly and bent down on one knee.

"Madame there's something about you, that I can't get off my mind," Sean sang at Polly. This startled her to the point she almost dropped her phone. She spotted Sean and begrudgingly smiled.

"I'd smack you if I weren't so glad to see you," Polly said to Sean, "How're you holding up?"

"Good. Can't wait to get to comic con!" Sean said with glee.

"Where's Danni?" Polly asked.

"Trying to develop telekinesis to pull myself over." Danni shouted.

"Fuck!" Sean swore as he ran back to Danni. He wheeled her to Polly.

"I'm so sorry!" Sean apologised.

"For every mistake, you'll owe me a drink." Danni said, smiling.

"Sold!" Sean agreed.

"Are you okay to compete today?" Polly asked Danni.

"Yeah; I messaged the contest organisers ahead of time. Leo is going to help me out from backstage." Danni answered. Leo came in and stood with them. He was dressed in regular but geeky clothes.

"Sean! Good to see you alive!" Leo greeted Sean.

"Shocking, I know." Sean said sarcastically.

"How are you?" Leo asked. Before Sean could answer, Jamie came rushing in in a costume from 'The Explorer.' They stopped between Leo and Sean.

"Hi all. Are we ready to go?" they said as they placed their arms around Leo and Sean. They broke away from Jamie's embrace and headed over to comic con together.

Chapter Nine

11:30am. The convention hall was busy but not over-crowded. There were a good number of business stalls and celebrity guest tables full of people queueing to get autographs. Every table was busy with activity. Sean, Leo, Jamie, Danni and Polly were queuing at the cosplay registration table. A cosplay crew member was registering people and taking their details. Leo was behind Danni's chair. Sean was glued to his phone, which kept getting messages from Alexia.

"Folks, I don't know if I can do this." Jamie fretted.

"Yes, you can. Your performance is wonderful!" Danni supported them.

"I'm going to be performing in front of the love of my life!" Jamie squeaked.

"And?" Polly challenged.

"What if I fuck up?"

"Do what Mal does - pretend like you were meant to do it and keep going." Leo advised.

"Really?" Jamie quizzed.

"You'd be shocked how often that works." Leo assured them.

"I'm so nervous." Jamie worried.

"We're all in this together. We all registered around the same time so hopefully we will be altogether in the queue." Polly tried to reassure Jamie.

"You'll have a personal cheerleader in me." Leo encouraged.

"Yeah?" Jamie asked.

"We'll all cheer for you, right Polly?"
Danni asked.

"Of course. Sean?" Polly waited for
Sean to agree but he was glued to his phone.
He was visually anxious and retreating into
himself.

"Earth to Sean?" Polly probed.

"What?" Sean snapped. Danni looked
at the time on her phone. It was 11:32am. She
turned to Sean.

"Is Alexia badgering you?" Leo asked
Sean.

"I'm fine." Sean said sharply.

"Sean, it's 11:32am. Do the thing."
Danni told Sean.

"Oh!" Sean said as he sent the photo
Danni sent earlier, pretending to Alexia that it
was his phone saying he had poor signal. Leo,
Polly and Jamie turned to Danni.

"I thought ahead." Danni explained.

"I'm impressed." Polly complimented. Sean put his phone in his pocket. The queue had gone down.

"Sorry everyone," Sean apologised.

"Don't worry," Jamie reassured Sean, "We'll keep you nice and occupied." As they waited, Michael came through to see the queue. He spotted the group. Jamie and Michael made eye contact. Michael checked the group out.

"Great costumes! I can't wait to spend more time with them later." Michael said flirtatiously. He left, leaving Jamie star struck. The others noticed this.

"Jamie?" Leo inquired.

"He noticed me." Jamie murmured. Polly got to the front of the queue.

"Hi!" Polly greeted the cosplay crew member in front of her.

"Hi there," The cosplay crew member greeted back, "Have you registered for our championship or are you signing up for our community contest?"

"Championship. I'm Polly Guilder. I'm cosplaying Samara from Lust at First Bite."

"Awesome! Let me check my list," The crew member said as she found Polly's name, "Yep! There you are. Make sure you're back by 2pm for pre-judging."

"Great. Thank you."

"No problem! See you later!" Polly stepped away from the queue. As Jamie signed up with the cosplay crew member, Polly spotted Mara talking to fans at her table. Polly thought about heading over but stopped herself. Her conflict over her feelings for Mara raged on in her torn heart.

The group had a mixed time in the next two and a half hours. Jamie was in a dream land state about their encounter with Michael whilst Polly was in an emotional quandary over Mara. Sean and Danni were having fun with the hint of flirtation ever hanging in the air.

"This will all end well," Leo sarcastically thought to himself as he saw what was going on around him. He kept to himself and avoided all temptation to make remarks. The group steadily made their way back to the cosplay area to join the queue for the contest. There was quite a group of competitors surrounding them in a variety of vividly imaginative costumes. The cosplay contest started in earnest 30 minutes later with Mal presenting on the stage. Polly, Jamie, Danni and Sean did their best to hold in their nerves.

"You'll all do great," Leo whispered to them as Mal introduced the judges to the stage.

"I am performing to more than just an audience," Jamie whispered back in a panic.

"I'm performing in front of *him*." Jamie pointed at Michael who strode confidently onto the stage.

"I know," Polly comforted them in a whisper, "But you've been practising like mad. You've got this."

"Just think - it'll be a few moments and then it's over." Sean added in a whisper. Jamie smiled back at them all. With that, the judges took their seats. Mal introduced Polly on to the stage. Polly walked confidently on to the stage, determined to keep her troubles behind the curtain. She embraced her moment on the stage and shone. As she performed to the crowd, Jamie became increasingly nervous knowing they were next. Danni kept her arm around them.

"You've got this," Danni whispered to Jamie, who smiled back at her. Polly finished their performance. As the crowd cheered and clapped, she went back to the queue backstage. She high fived Leo, Danni, Sean and Jamie individually before running to the back of the queue. Jamie was announced as the next contestant to perform. They hesitated for a moment before running on stage. Danni, Leo and Sean watched intently as Jamie performed their speech. Midway through, Leo started getting Danni's wheelchair ready.

"Ready?" Leo whispered to Danni.

"Absolutely." Danni whispered back.

"Good luck. You've got this." Sean whispered to Danni. Danni turned to face Sean and smiled at him. Their moment was broken by the applause and cheers Jamie received for their performance. They were visibly exhilarated as they high-fived Leo, Sean and Danni. They ran to the back of the queue.

Leo took Danni out onto the stage as she was announced. Sean kept his eyes squarely on Danni throughout her performance. Time melted away as he saw her make the audience laugh with her stand-up routine. He was enamoured with her presence. He didn't even notice Leo coming back to stand with him.

"Dude, you okay?" Leo whispered to Sean. Sean snapped out of it and turned to Leo.

"I'm fine," Sean whispered, "Just trying to remember my bit."

"If you say so." Leo whispered. With that, Danni's performance was over. Leo came back to take her off the stage. As they came back, Danni squeezed Sean's hand before they left for the back of the queue.

An hour elapsed. Polly was holding her trophy and certificate as she, Leo, Mal, Jamie, Danni and Sean reached the outside of the Glyndŵr hotel. Leo and Mal were linking arms. Jamie was pushing Danni in her wheelchair. Sean was distracted by his phone.

"Well done again, Polly," Danni congratulated her.

"Yeah, you were amazing." Jamie jumped in.

"So, Polly, now that we're firmly away from the con floor: who are you taking to the after party?" Mal asked.

"Are you and Leo already going?" Polly asked.

"Yeah we're covered. You just have to choose between Sean, Danni or Jamie." Leo informed her. Polly turned to face Jamie, Sean and Danni. Jamie looked hopeful.

"You'll have to eliminate me. The venue isn't accessible to me." Danni told Polly. Sean's attention deviated from his phone to Danni.

"What?" Sean quizzed.

"I can't be Polly's plus 1. I can't access the building." Danni explained.

"What? I was told it was accessible." Mal said.

"Their idea of access is half a staircase of steps." Danni confirmed.

"I'm going to have words with the party organisers," Mal sighed, irritated, "That's just fucking ridiculous. I'm so sorry Danni."

"It's okay. I'm sure Jamie wants to go more than me anyway." Danni assured Mal.

"Jamie?" Polly asked Jamie. Jamie smiled, elated.

"I love you, Polly." Jamie squeaked.

"You better. Shall we meet here at 8pm?" Polly asked the group.

"Sure! I've got to get ready." Jamie immediately ran back into the hotel, having forgotten to apply the brakes to Danni's wheelchair. She started to slowly roll backwards until Sean grabbed the chair handles.

Chapter Ten

8pm came around. Danni, Sean, Mal, Leo and Polly were sitting at a bar table together with a drink each. They were all dressed in regular clothes.

"So, Danni & Sean: what are you two going to do?" Mal asked in a vaguely suggestive manner.

"We can probably just drink, chat and chill with crap TV." Sean answered, ignoring Mal's tone entirely.

"I'm not sure I brought enough booze with me." Danni admitted.

"I'll run to the supermarket after this to make sure we do." Sean told her.

Mara suddenly came into the bar area. She spotted Polly with the rest of the gang. She approached Polly, who became a little uncomfortable but was secretly happy to see her.

"Hey" Mara greeted Polly.

"Hey" Polly returned the greeting.

"I heard you won the cosplay contest today. I just wanted to say well done."

"Thanks."

By now the sexual tension between the two was clear to everyone around them.

"Hey Mara. Did you have a good day?" Leo asked, keen to break the tension.

"Yeah it was decent," Mara replied. "Are you all going to the after party?"

"Polly is, with Leo, Jamie & I" Mal responded.

"Cool. Maybe I'll see you there?" Mara said to Polly.

"Yeah." Polly smiled at her. With that, Mara left.

"Remind me: why didn't you pursue anything with her?" Danni asked Polly.

"You're clearly into her." Leo pointed out.

"Yeah I'm into her. That's the problem and I don't want to talk about it." Polly said rapidly.

"We'll back off," Mal reassured her.

"Please do." Polly snapped. Jamie came to the bar area dressed in a casual suit.

"Someone's on the pull" Leo remarked.

"I'm a one-man person," Jamie declared. "Shall we go?"

"Will you two be okay?" Polly asked Sean & Danni.

"I think we'll be alright." Sean answered. He and Danni smiled at each other, besotted. Polly, Mal and Leo finished their drinks and placed their glasses on the bar.

"Alright. We're off, losers." Polly announced.

"Don't have too much fun without us." said Mal.

"We'll try," Danni teased.

Forty-five minutes later, Jamie, Polly, Mal and Leo arrived at the Glyndŵr Comic Con after party. It was a somewhat sparse affair with a make-shift bar manned by a lone bartender. There were several people in cosplay hanging out. Michael was with some friends. It was an almost dank atmosphere. There was nothing particularly special about the environment itself and nothing that really created a real party feel.

"Well, this looks promising." Leo
sarcastically remarked.

"That's what our concealed flasks are
for." Jamie pointed out.

"How do they get away with charging
extra for this tripe?" Polly enquired.

"I think it largely pays for the bar."
Mal suggested.

"That thing?" Jamie pointed at the
bar, a little aggrieved.

"This is an improvement on the last
one," Leo explained.

"Shall we get us some drinks?" Mal
asked the group.

"I'll get this round. Beers all round?"
Polly queried. The others all nodded. Polly
went to the bar and waited to be served. She
saw Mara waiting too. She considered going
over to her but didn't. She looked at Mara

again. She was about to go over when the bartender grabbed her attention.

"What can I get you, Miss?" the bartender asked her.

"Four bottles of your cheapest beer." Polly answered. Mara looked over and saw Polly ordering.

"Coming up!" said the bartender. Mara headed over to Polly.

"Hey," Mara greeted Polly.

"Hey" Polly responded.

"You okay?"

"I'll feel better with a little overpriced, crap beer in me."

"That's something." The bartender handed over four bottles of beer to Polly.

"That'll be £20.60." The bartender told her. Polly went into her wallet and handed the bartender her credit card.

"It's contactless." She told them.

"Perfect!" The bartender exclaimed. The bartender completed the transaction and handed Polly her credit card back. When she turned back, Mara was still there.

"I have to get these beers to my friends then I'll be right back." Polly told Mara.

"Okay." Mara smiled at her. Polly took the beers and left the bar.

Danni was sitting on the bed of the hotel room she was sharing with Sean. She looked at herself in the mirror. She started to brush her hair and put some lip gloss on. At that moment, she heard the door start to unlock. She threw the lip gloss on to the table and sat back on the edge of the bed. Sean came through the door with two carrier bags of alcohol, snacks and mixers.

"I have supplies," he triumphantly announced as he placed the bags on the table.

"Excellent!" Danni said.

"I should check my phone before Alexia starts calling me." Sean sat on the bed next to Danni.

Danni got up and started getting out the alcohol and mixers.

"Did you text her back when we got back to the hotel?" she asked.

Sean started to check his phone. There were many messages from Alexia getting increasingly agitated. Danni turned to face him.

"I did," he answered, "It didn't seem to help. All she seems fixated on is how I didn't message her."

"Doesn't she think you had no signal all day?"

"Yes but apparently I'm terrible for not inventing an additional phone mast." Sean was still glued to his phone.

Danni turned away from him and sighed. She dug out the plastic cups and started mixing a cocktail. As she was preparing, Sean's phone went off. He answered it.

"Alexia I was just -" Sean started.

"Why didn't you answer me?" Alexia interrupted angrily.

"Look, I couldn't do anything about the signal today."

"That's not good enough. You should've answered me."

"What do you want me to do: erect a mast out of thin air. Because -"

"Don't insult me!"

"I'm not insulting you".

"I want to know what you were doing that made responding to me unimportant."

"I wasn't doing anything. I was -" Sean started as his phone died. He checked his phone to see the battery had died.

"Shit!" Sean yelled. The sudden loud noise shocked Danni to spill part of the drink she was making.

"Danni! Are you okay?" Sean asked as she went to the bathroom to wash her hand.

"I'm fine," she told him, "I just spilt some of the drink."

"I'm sorry" Sean said.

"Do me a favour?" Danni asked as she came out of the bathroom, "Don't charge

your phone; just grab a drink. Let's get
pissed."

    "Honestly? That sounds amazing."
Sean smiled at Danni.

Chapter Eleven

Polly headed for Leo, Mal and Jamie with the beers. They each took a beer from her.

"Folks I -" Polly started.

"We saw." Leo interrupted her.

"Go after her, you fool!" Jamie exalted.

"Jamie, this isn't a rom-com, but I agree: fuck off Polly." Leo chimed in.

"I love you too." Polly joked. She went back to Mara at the bar. Mal, Leo and Jamie clink their beer bottles.

Michael came over. Jamie blushed and sipped beer.

"Mal! Good to see you again," Michael greeted.

"Michael! Have I introduced you to my husband Leo?" Mal greeted him.

"You haven't," Michael confirmed, "Good to meet you."

"You too," Leo smiled back at him, "I believe you met my friend Jamie." Michael turned to face Jamie. There was a definite attraction between them.

"Did I see you earlier at the cosplay contest?" Michael asked Jamie.

"Yeah. I was cosplaying The Explorer from Season 10, Episode 6. It was pre goo." Jamie explained.

"Ah! I remember. Your stitch job on the jacket was flawless."

"Yeah?"

"Oh yeah, it was amazing. So was your handle of the Taal Van Twee speech. How did you master that?"

"My grandmother is Dutch. She's been teaching me."

"Fascinating." Michael and Jamie smiled at each other. Jamie was in heaven.

"We're going to take a turn about the room." Mal told them. He linked arms with Leo, and they walked off. Michael and Jamie kept talking to each other.

"Why are we leaving?" Leo asked when out of ear shot of Michael and Jamie.

"Soon enough Michael will turn the charm on, and I don't need to be there for it." Mal explained.

"I hope Jamie doesn't get the wrong end of the stick." Leo worried. They walked past the bar where Mara and Polly were talking to each other. They were physically close.

"I hate to break a good mood, but we need to address the elephant in the room." Mara directly told Polly.

"Yeah," Polly agreed as she fiddled with her own hair, "I like you. I like you quite a bit and sex with you was beyond phenomenal."

"I sense a 'but' coming."

"But I'm really confused by all this. I've never been with anyone who wasn't a cis man before and I wasn't expecting that to change."

"Does that mean you don't want to see me?"

"No! It's not that. I don't know what to do."

"I get it." Mara sighed.

"Yeah?" Polly wondered.

"I'll give you space." Mara started to leave but Polly stopped her.

"We can still hang out tonight, right?" Polly asked.

"I don't want something to happen then you avoid me again. Sort out how you feel then we'll revisit whatever this is." Mara left abruptly. Polly felt stung, but she understood.

A little time had passed by. Sean was preparing another drink whilst Danni sat on the bed.

"I wonder how the others are." Danni pondered aloud.

"I'm sure they're having a blast." Sean said.

"How're you feeling?"

"Slightly less dizzy. Why did we chug our last drink?" Sean groaned.

"You challenged me. Never ever do that."

"You think I can't take you?" The sexual tension between them was building.

"You want to go again?" Danni teased him. Sean turned to face Danni with drinks in each hand.

"Now we don't want to go too hard, too fast," Sean teased back, "We can take it slow for a while." He handed her her drink. Their hands brushed gently.

"I suppose we have to be good sometimes." Danni said, pretending to sulk. Sean sat on the bed next to her. He raised his glass.

"To a comic con I had real fun at!" Sean proclaimed.

148

"To comic con!" Danni proclaimed too as they clinked their plastic glasses. They took a sip of their drinks.

"I forgot how nice it can be just to be with my friends," Sean sighed happily.

"You should do it more often," Danni gently pointed out.

"It doesn't help that you all live so far away."

"I can't believe you two moved to Wichama. It's so straight I'm practically allergic to it."

"Isn't it appropriate that the token straight couple live in Straightsville?"

"I guess." Danni took a sip of her drink. She tapped her finger on the plastic cup awkwardly. There was a distinct romantic and sexual tension building between the pair but now they seemed aware of it.

"If we're going to get drunk, we may as well do it properly." Sean decided.

"What do you mean?" Danni asked.

"How about a game of 'I Have Never'?" Sean proposed. She smirked at him.

Mal and Leo stood together watching the other attendees. Michael and Jamie were clearly flirting with each other whilst Polly sat alone at the bar.

"Why do we always end up watching people at these parties?" Mal asked Leo.

"Because we're married, the booze is too expensive and we're introverts?" Leo proposed.

"Good point." Mal conceded. Leo spotted Polly at the bar.

"Shit, Polly is on her own." said Leo.

"I'm not surprised," said Mal, "Mara doesn't need to be messed around."

"The question remains: will Polly figure herself out enough in time?"

"Are you the narrator now?"

A loud laugh was heard. It was coming from Michael and Jamie.

"At least one of our friends is having fun." Mal pointed out. Michael and Jamie were continuing to talk to each other flirtatiously.

"So, Jamie, are you seeing anyone?" Michael asked them.

"No. You?" Jamie asked hopefully.

"Nothing serious. I'm not the commitment type."

"Oh."

"I'm not looking for a relationship. I'm looking for fun."

"Do you think you can have fun with me?"

Michael stroked Jamie's cheek.

"Are you offering some fun?" He asked in a sultry tone.

"Yes." Jamie whispered back. With that, Michael and Jamie began to make out. It became more intense the longer it went on, the two clinging onto each other for dear life. Once they stopped making out, Michael kissed Jamie's ear.

"Follow me," Michael whispered to them. They held hands and rushed off.

Danni and Sean were sitting opposite each other on the bed.

"Okay if you don't get the other person to drink, you must drink yourself." Danni proposed.

"Got it." Sean agreed.

"Alright: I have never been in a monogamous relationship."

"Oh, you bitch," Sean complained as he drank from his cup. "Alright: I have never been in a *non*-monogamous relationship."

"Blast!" Danni complained as she drank. "I have never broken a bone during sex."

"Fuck me," Sean griped. Danni giggled at him as he drank from his cup. "I have never used a mobility aid as a weapon."

"I'll proudly drink to that achievement. The bastard shouldn't have tried to slap my arse." Danni declared as she drank from her cup. "I have never been trapped in a lift." Sean took a drink from his cup.

"I have never thrown up on a rollercoaster." Sean said. Danni drank.

"I have never forgotten my lines during a cosplay contest performance." Danni accused. Sean hesitated for a moment then took a drink from his cup.

"I have never gotten a tattoo." Sean indicted. Danni drank again.

"I have never had a one-night stand." Sean continued.

"I have never sent a nude to the wrong person." Danni fired back.

"I have never done the walk of shame."

"I have never had sex with a close friend." Danni and Sean looked at each other, looked at their drinks, then chugged them.

Chapter Twelve

Danni was preparing another drink. Sean looked at his phone. He contemplated charging it until he looked at Danni. He smiled and put his phone away instead. He headed over to Danni and cuddled her from behind.

"Cocktail lady, where's my drink?" Sean asked.

"It's coming, you impatient drunk." Danni giggled.

"I'm not drunk." Sean argued.

"'I'm not drunk.'" Danni mocked him. She put down the prepared drinks. Sean tickled her. Danni had to stop herself falling onto the poured drinks as she giggled. She turned to face Sean. They felt a surge of romantic tension fill the room. Sean placed his hand on her cheek.

"What are we doing?" Sean asked tenderly.

"I don't know," Danni admitted, "Do you want to stop?"

"No," Sean replied.

The tension became too much: they kissed. Their kiss was tender and kind. They stopped for a moment before launching into a passionate embrace.

Sean unbuttoned Danni's shirt. He took off his own shirt. He brought Danni back into him and kissed her neck. One of his hands grasped her breast. The other was sliding up her skirt. Sean began to play with Danni who started to moan with aroused excitement.

Danni reached for Sean's zipper. She pulled it down and placed her hand through. As she started to play with Sean they both became more sexually excited as they mutually masturbated each other.

They eventually separated from each other, quickly undressed and climbed on to the bed. Sean spooned Danni from behind and started to have sex with her. He reached over with his free hand to stimulate her clitoris. Danni was thrown into peak sexual enjoyment as she moved in tandem with Sean.

Danni eventually began to climax. This aroused Sean to the point of orgasm himself. As he did so, he bit into Danni's shoulder. This excited her more as she continued to orgasm.

As they lay exhausted, Sean held Danni closer to him and kissed her neck tenderly. She turned to face him. Sean brought her into a passionate kiss. They stayed close together as they panted.

Michael and Jamie headed into the after-party toilets together. Michael locked the door behind him and smiled at Jamie, who was very visibly excited.

Michael went to Jamie, swept them into a hold and started to make out with them. He moved his hand down Jamie's chest and towards their trousers. Michael unbuttoned Jamie's trousers, so they fell to the ground, then slid their underwear off. He started to give Jamie a hand job.

Jamie became excited as they were played with. They clung to Michael's shoulders and kissed his neck. Michael hoisted Jamie so their crotch was just above his.

He unzipped his trousers and leaned Jamie against a wall. Michael and Jamie began to have sex against the toilet wall. Jamie moved their hips in tandem with Michael. They were both getting hotter and hotter as the sex continued. Michael was thrusting into Jamie when he abruptly orgasmed,groaning loudly as he did so. He stopped thrusting and leaned his head against Jamie's shoulder.

Michael pulled out from Jamie and started to wash himself up. Jamie tidied themselves up and picked up their trousers and underwear. Michael zipped up his trousers.

"That was fun. Thanks." Michael said as he left. Jamie stood in the toilet confused by how they were feeling. They'd always wanted to get with Michael, so why did it feel so hollow?

Polly went into her hotel room. She checked her phone and saw a goodnight text from Mara on her phone. She started to feel a little excited.

She headed for her suitcase. She opened it and found her Unbound Squish sex toy. She pulled her underpants off from under her dress.

She sat on her bed; legs spread apart. Polly squeezed her Squish and placed it under her dress to play with herself. She started to get increasingly aroused. With her free hand, Polly played with herself more. She was in ecstasy as she cried out.

"Oh fuck, Mara!" she gasped. She continued to pleasure herself until she started to reach orgasm. She was exhausted as she finished. At that moment, a wave of realisation washed over her: she realised she was very much into Mara no matter what she did to deny it. She headed into the bathroom to get some toilet roll and sighed as she tidied herself up.

Five weeks after the events of Glyndŵr Comic Con, Polly was sitting in her bedroom starting up her computer. She looked at her phone and saw she had no messages. She sighed.

She looked at her computer. She tapped on her mouse. She contemplated her next move as she browsed on social media.

She encountered one of Mara's profiles. She took a deep breath.

"Maybe if I just write to her?" Polly thought to herself. She pressed on the 'New Message' icon and stared at it. She struggled to know what to write. A message suddenly appeared on Polly's phone. It was from Jamie: 'Can we talk? I need to talk to you about something.'. Polly tapped on her phone.

"Fuck it," she muttered to herself as she texted Jamie back. She put her phone on her table and turned her attention back to the computer. She had just started to type when Jamie called her.

"Shit." she muttered as she answered the phone.

"Hey. What's up?" Polly asked Jamie.

162

"Dude, Sean is avoiding Danni."
Jamie told her.

"What? Why?"

"You can't tell anyone."

"I won't."

"Danni and Sean slept together that
night at Glyndŵr Comic Con whilst we were
at the after party." Jamie said.

"Shit! Now Sean's avoiding her out of
guilt?"

"I suspect so."

"I'll kill him for hurting Danni." Polly
fumed.

"No! I promised Danni I wouldn't
tell."

"Okay."

"How are we going to handle this
weekend?"

"Danni is competing this weekend so at least they'll be apart for a good chunk of it," Polly mused. "Are you happy to cling to Alexia a bit?"

"I do need to track down Michael at some point." Jamie replied.

"I thought he wasn't interested in anything serious."

"He said that, but we clicked. Guys always play hard to get."

Polly grimaced.

"Okay, I would go into everything that's wrong with what you've just said but I need you on side this weekend. We'll put a pin in that."

"Great."

"Let's brief Mr & Mr Knight for backup," Polly suggested.

"I'll do it. If I don't speak to you sooner I'll see you at con."

"Alright. See you at con."

Chapter Thirteen

Wichama Comic Con had a long
queue waiting to get in. Outside and inside of
the comic con were both incredibly busy with
lots of cosplaying and non-cosplaying
customers around. The shops and artist alley
tables were busy with people crowding them
to buy merchandise. The queues for the
celebrity guests were lengthy.

Polly, Jamie and Leo were all dressed
in costumes: Polly was dressed as a ghostly
nurse called Zelda from 'Nurse Limbo', Leo
was dressed as a vampiric character from
'Lust At First Bite' and Jamie was dressed in
the same 'The Explorer' costume they wore
at Glyndŵr Comic Con. They all looked
around.

"Have you seen Mr & Mrs Hetero Dysfunction?" Leo asked.

"No. They came from home today." Jamie told him.

"Has anyone seen Danni & Reuben?" Polly enquired.

"No but I know they're already inside. Danni had to make sure the competition was accessible." Leo answered.

"What if they bump into each other?" Jamie worried.

"I texted Reuben. He's on it." Jamie confirmed.

Meanwhile inside the comic con, Alexia and Sean were dressed once more as Super Ginge and Heidi Gertrude Duff from 'Super Ginge.' They were exploring the Artists' Alley when they came across Mara. Sean smiled and waved at her.

"Hey Mara," Sean greeted Mara, "How're you?"

"Yeah not bad mate," Mara greeted him back, "Sean, right?"

"Yeah. Well remembered." Sean affirmed. Alexia cleared her throat intently.

"And since *when* did you know each other?" Alexia demanded. The atmosphere became awkward.

"Alexia, this is Mara. She writes the Sara-Fi comics. We met in person at Glyndŵr Comic Con." Sean explained.

"I thought we weren't going to mention that con!" Alexia snapped.

"But -" Sean started.

"I didn't get to go, and you ignored me. You're lucky I forgave you." Alexia snidely retorted. Sean took a deep breath and turned to Alexia with a forced smile.

"You know what? I need the toilet. Why don't you check out Mara's work whilst I go pee?" he said. Before Alexia could answer, Sean left.

Five minutes later, Polly, Leo and Jamie had got into the comic con. They bumped into Sean, who looked incredibly tense.

"You look dreadful." Polly remarked.

"Thanks Polly." Sean answered sarcastically.

"What happened to you?" Leo asked Sean.

"Alexia is winding me up." Sean elucidated.

"You haven't seen Danni or Reuben, have you?" Jamie asked gingerly.

"No." Sean snapped.

"Dude, chill." Polly warned Sean.

"Don't tell me to chill." Sean rudely replied.

"Just because you can't keep it in your trousers doesn't mean you can take it out on me." Jamie snapped at Sean. He looked at Polly and Leo then turned to Jamie.

"I was worried you and Danni would end up shagging and she'd get hurt because you don't have the balls to leave Alexia," Polly chimed in.

"That's fucking rich coming from the person who led a woman on because she can't accept she isn't straight anymore." Sean barked.

"Sean -" Jamie started.

"You're in no position to talk," Sean interrupted, "You tricked a guy into sleeping with you as a challenge so you can fulfil your romantic delusion. Newsflash: rom-coms aren't fucking real, Jamie."

"That's it." Leo said as he got in between Polly, Jamie and Sean. He faced Sean.

"Seeing as I'm your only friend right now, I'm staying with you," Leo told Sean. He turned to face Polly and Jamie, "You two: calm the fuck down. Yelling at Sean because he's struggling to leave an abusive situation isn't going to help. He sucks for hurting Danni but let's not paint him as the villain."

Polly and Jamie stormed off together. Leo faced Sean who put his head into his hands.

"Thanks, Leo," Sean said as he raised his head from his hands.

"Do you need to go outside?" Leo asked gently.

"Alexia will get suspicious if I don't try and" Sean's words trailed off as Alexia came rushing over. She immediately clung to Sean.

"Back from the toilet I see." Alexia said snidely.

"It's my fault," Leo stepped in, "I bumped into him."

"Yeah. Anyway, that Michael guy is going to do a talk on The Explorer cosplay in half an hour. We're going." Alexia said through gritted teeth. She dragged Sean away, Leo following behind.

In the meantime, Polly and Jamie briefly looked back to see Alexia with Leo and Sean. They both sighed in disgust.

"I can't believe Sean yelled at us like that." Jamie complained.

"He may have been an arsehole about it, but he wasn't totally wrong." Polly conceded.

"What?!"

"I messed Mara around because I was struggling to figure myself out."

"You're going through something huge. He can't criticise you for that."

"I didn't need to hurt a decent person because of it."

"I mean -" Jamie tailed off as they saw Michael alone. In that moment, Polly was spurred into action,

"I'm sorry. I have to go." Jamie apologised.

"Me too," said Polly. She rushed away on a mission.

Jamie approached Michael. He noticed and seemed hesitant to see them.

"Hi there," Michael greeted, "Jamie, right?"

"Yeah." Jamie smiled.

"I have to prepare for a talk soon." Michael tried to leave but Jamie stopped him.

"Why didn't you message me?" Jamie asked. Michael faced Jamie, perplexed.

"What?"

"We had sex. I thought you'd message me to follow up for a date or something."

"I thought I told you I was just looking for fun."

"Yeah but -"

"Did you just say 'but'?" Michael asked, indignantly. Jamie hesitated, unsure what to say.

"Great: another super fan who saw my "just want fun" boundary as a fucking challenge to get me." Michael sighed, irritated.

"But you used me." Jamie accused him.

"I'll make this easy: when I said I was looking for fun, that's exactly it. If anyone used anyone, you used me. I don't know why, and I don't want to know."

"Michael -"

"Leave me alone." Michael interrupted as he left.

Polly wandered the comic con, searching for Artists' Alley.

She was two tables away from Mara's table, which was quiet until two burly strangers approached.

"You're one of them trannies, ain't you?" The first one accused Mara.

"Fucking disgusting," The second spat, "They let you near kiddies at a family event?!"

"We don't need your kind here," the first transphobe interjected, "Get out before I beat you out." Mara stood still, unsure what to do. She didn't spot Polly coming over, angry at what was being said.

"I'll get security if you don't leave." Mara warned.

"My mate said you need to fuck off," The second man said. He grabbed Mara by the shirt.

"Hey!" A shout could be heard. It was Polly who dragged the first bully to the ground. The second one let go of Mara and went to hit Polly. She dodged the hit and kicked him in the stomach. The artist next to Mara went to comfort her.

"Stay the fuck away from my girlfriend or I'll beat you both to a pulp." Polly yelled at them.

"Someone get security!" one of the transphobes cried.

"They're on the way to kick you out for assaulting a stall holder. Good luck coming back again." said the artist hugging Mara. At that moment, two security guards came and marched the transphobes away. Polly faced Mara.

"Are you okay?" The artist asked Mara.

"Yeah. Thanks, Ian," Mara replied.

"Mara?" Polly sheepishly approached her.

"Hey. Thanks for that." Mara said.

"Don't thank me. I'm sorry. I messed you around whilst trying to find myself. I know I don't deserve it but if you'll have me, I'm ready. I want to be with you." Polly said.

Mara stepped over to Polly and pulled her into a kiss. The artists around them broke out in applause.

"I knew you'd come around." Mara smirked.

"I would love to stay here and make out with you, but I do need to head to the cosplay desk to register."

"Mara, I'll cover you. Go have a break for as long as you need." Ian offered. Mara chucked keys at him.

"Thanks. Those are for the cash drawer. I'll be back in a bit." Mara smiled.

Chapter Fourteen

2pm came by. Polly finished registering for the cosplay contest. She went back over to Mara and held her hand.

Jamie came by. They initially didn't notice Mara and Polly holding hands.

"Jamie! How did it go with Michael?" Polly enquired.

"I don't want to talk about it." Jamie answered sulkily.

"Okay I won't ask." Polly accepted.

Jamie noticed Polly and Mara holding hands. They smiled.

"Shit, you two are together now?" Jamie asked excitedly.

"Yeah." Mara confirmed with a smile.

"Yes! Finally! At least one of us gets a happy ending." Jamie squealed.

"I like this one. They're sweet." Mara said of Jamie.

"Jamie, I need to go get into the queue. Why don't you and Mara head in and get some seats?" Polly suggested.

"Sure! If you see Reuben and Danni, give them giant hugs from me." Jamie asked.

"Will do!" Polly kissed Mara before she left. Jamie offered their arm to link with Mara.

"I need a cheering up and nothing quite does it like a good love story." Jamie asked Mara.

"Okay," Mara agreed. She linked arms with Jamie. They headed to the cosplay stage area, which was relatively empty. They took two seats in an empty row.

"So, tell me how you two finally got together." Jamie requested.

"Well -" Mara started.

"Mara! Jamie!" A loud voice shouted. They turned to face Leo who was with Sean and Alexia.

"Hi! Leo, right?" Mara quizzed Leo.

"Yeah. Mind if we sit with you?" Leo requested politely.

"Not at all." Mara accepted. Leo sat next to Mara whilst Alexia and Sean sat in front of them. Sean turned to face Mara, but Alexia kissed him.

"C'mon baby," Alexia cooed, "The show will start soon." The others shuffled uncomfortably.

Meanwhile in the cosplay backstage area, Polly was in the queue. Three spaces ahead she spotted Danni cosplaying Sara-Fi from 'Sara-Fi' in her wheelchair and Reuben cosplaying a Coffee Shop Employee from 'Coffee Shop: The Musical'. Polly turned to the person behind her cosplaying Super Ginge from 'Super Ginge.'

"Can you save my spot? I need to see my friends quickly." Polly asked politely. The Super Ginge cosplayer nodded. Polly went to Danni and Reuben.

"Hey." Polly said to Reuben and Danni.

"Polly!" Reuben greeted as she hugged him. She then hugged Danni.

"Stupid question: how are you, Danni?" Polly enquired.

"I just want to compete then head home," Danni said quickly.

"We'd love to hang out with you for a bit before you go." Polly suggested.

"Will Sean be there?" Reuben asked tensely.

"I doubt it. Alexia has him on a shorter lead than usual." Polly confessed.

"If she starts any trouble I won't have it." Reuben warned.

"Reuben -" Danni started.

"It's bad enough you won't let me punch Sean for hurting you this way. Can I at least yell at Alexia?" Reuben interrupted.

"If you want," Danni sighed, defeated.

"Leo has been stuck with them all day so he may start a religion after you if you do," Polly told Reuben.

"Poor him," Reuben commiserated. A bell was heard.

"I better get back in the queue. Good luck. You'll both nail it," Polly told them.

"Thanks, Polly." Danni said.

"Good luck," Reuben wished Polly.

Polly went back to her place in the queue.

An hour and the contest passed by. Alexia, Sean, Mara, Leo and Jamie were waiting around outside the cosplay stage area.

"That was amazing," Mara enthused, "I didn't realise what I was missing before."

"Yeah they're great even when a twat judges them." Jamie sulked.

"Jamie -" Leo reprimanded Jamie. Reuben arrived alone. He made brief eye contact with Sean and quickly turned to Leo, Jamie and Mara.

"Reuben! We missed you. Where's Danni?" Jamie asked.

"Polly is bringing her once Danni sorts the prize money," Reuben explained.

"You and Polly were great, but Danni deserved that win. Right folks?" Leo asked the group.

"Totally! I was blown away by her grasp of the character," Mara complimented.

"She nearly made me cry, the bitch," Jamie jokingly complained.

"You?" Reuben challenged Sean. Sean hesitated for a moment whilst Alexia glared at him.

"She was amazing," he blurted out, "Then again she always is." Alexia squeezed his arm.

"Alexia, what did -?" Leo started.

"All hail the Champion Queen!" Polly shouted as she wheeled Danni towards them. Danni was smiling holding her trophy. Sean became excited and anxious to see Danni again.

"I can't describe how cool it was to watch you bring Sara to life!" Mara complimented Danni.

"Thanks, Mara! I'm glad I did it some justice," Danni accepted.

"I've got to go pack up but if you're all around later we could hang out before I leave?" Mara proposed.

"You better believe it." Polly approved. Mara blew a kiss at Polly as she walked away.

Leo turned to face Polly as Mal approached the group.

"I'm just going to say this: fucking finally." Leo said.

"I'll take that as a compliment." Polly smiled. Mal stood by Leo.

"Oh good: everyone's here. We've got a bit of an announcement." Mal said.

"For our 5th wedding anniversary in a few months' time, we're having a vow renewal ceremony." Leo announced to the group. Alexia scowled at Sean whilst the rest of the group erupted in cheers.

Chapter Fifteen

"Congratulations!" Danni said, smiling warmly at Leo and Mal.

"This is amazing!" said Jamie.

"Brilliant stuff," agreed Reuben.

"Why haven't *you* proposed, Sean?" Alexia demanded. The atmosphere became far more tense. Polly and Reuben swapped places.

Alexia let go of Sean's arm and turned to face him with her arms folded stroppily. Sean was intensely uncomfortable.

"It's been 8 years. Why haven't you proposed to me yet?" Alexia pushed.

"Alexia, can we not talk about this right now? I'm not comfortable doing this." Sean pleaded.

"For fuck's sake, I'll do it." Alexia said as she got down on one knee. Mal and Leo covered their faces with their hands. Danni was shocked at what she was witnessing. Jamie suddenly had a realisation about their own behaviour around Michael as they saw him in the distance.

"Alexia -" Sean started.

"It always seems impossible until it's done. Seeing as you won't propose to me, I have to do it to you so we can get planning." Alexia said forcefully.

Sean was stuck in place. His anxiety was sky high. Danni, hurt by what she was watching, tapped Reuben's hand.

"We're leaving," she whispered. Reuben clutched Danni's wheelchair and they quickly left. Danni could barely contain herself.

After a near millennium of hesitation, Sean couldn't take any more.

"Alexia, I can't do this." Sean blurted out. He looked to see that Danni and Reuben were gone. He tensed himself up further and started to run in their direction.

Jamie took the opportunity to leave themself. They approached Michael, who was on his own.

"Michael?" Jamie hesitantly asked. Michael turned to see Jamie. He was about to turn back.

"I want to apologise." Jamie elaborated. Michael turned to face Jamie, surprised.

"I have this fantasy in my head. I want the perfect romance you see in the movies. I want the butterflies, the intrigue and the romantic pay-off. The thing is I saw your boundary as a challenge. That was wrong. I'm so sorry.

"What you did was really fucked," Michael sighed, "I do appreciate you apologising."

"I need to work on myself before I can be with anyone. I do hope in the future we can be friends." Jamie continued.

"Maybe." Michael smiled at them. Jamie smiled back.

They turned to see Danni, Reuben and Sean were missing from the group. They turned back to Michael.

"I have to go," Jamie explained, "See you around."

"See you around." Michael agreed.

Reuben stopped the wheelchair, not realising Sean was coming after them. He put the brakes on the wheelchair and crouched down to hug Danni.

"I'm sorry, Danni," he said gently.

"You didn't do anything wrong," Danni responded.

"I know." Reuben said as he broke away from the hug. He looked up to see Sean coming. He stood back up.

"What do you want, Sean?" Reuben asked, irritated. Sean ran past him and faced Danni.

"I have nothing to say to you." Danni said coldly.

"Danni, I'm sorry. I didn't mean -"

"I don't want to hear 'I didn't mean to hurt you'," Danni interrupted. "It doesn't matter because you already did it, Sean."

"I have feelings for you, Danni." Sean blurted out. There was a pregnant pause in the air as no one quite knew what to do. Sean gathered himself.

"When I'm around you I'm so happy. I go crazy not being able to touch you." He continued.

"I have feelings for you too, but I didn't fuck you over." Danni threw back at Sean.

"I'm stuck." Sean complained.

"Sean, I feel awful you're in the situation you are in with Alexia. I really do. That still doesn't justify fucking me then dumping me like trash," Danni said firmly.

Polly appeared suddenly.

"I'm so sorry to do this but Mal, Leo and Jamie probably can't hold up Alexia for much longer." Polly warned the trio.

"Reuben, we're going."

Reuben stepped behind Danni and took the brakes off her wheelchair. Danni looked at Sean one more time but looked away again as she and Reuben left.

Alexia arrived, enraged.

"You went running after Danni?! She's a retarded tramp who trapped a pathetic -" Alexia started. She caught herself mid-rant. Polly looked to Sean to respond. He was horrified at what he had just heard.

"Sean, I didn't mean that," Alexia panicked. "What I mean is . . . look, forget it. It'll all be fine once we're married -"

"That's enough." Sean angrily interrupted, stunning both Polly and Alexia.

"I've had enough of your toxic nonsense," Sean yelled at Alexia. "I've had enough of the abusive texts and screaming phone calls. I've had enough of you bullying me into anything and everything you want. I don't know what sort of fucking box you're trying to fit me into, but newsflash: I don't fit. I'll get my stuff and then I never want to see your face again."

Polly put her arm around Sean. Sean felt both liberated and claustrophobic at the same time. It was a long time coming but he was acting on an impulse. Polly and Sean started walking away together.

Alexia, panicked at being dumped, tried to stop him by grabbing his free arm. Polly saw this and pushed her violently to the ground.

"I'll come and get Sean's possessions. One bit of trouble from you and I'll ring the Police." Polly growled at Alexia. Polly and Sean kept walking. Alexia stood up from the ground.

"You can't leave me! You need me! Don't leave. Sean!" Alexia screamed at him. Sean was frightened but continued to walk away with Polly.

Epilogue

It was a few months later in the bright but cold Brighthelmstone. Outside the Brighthelmstone hotel, a collection of wedding guests were arriving at the hotel in formal attire. The hotel itself was rather grand with ornate decorations all around. There was a sign outside pointing to The Pavilion Suite that said, "The Knight Reception."

Inside the Pavilion Suite was a vast array of guests. There was finger food spread across four tables. A make-shift bar was in operation next to it with a bartender serving drinks to attendees. There were a number of people chatting and having fun. Leo and Mal were chatting to Michael and Jamie. Ariana and Sean were with Polly and Mara, who were holding hands. Reuben and Danni were chatting together while eating. Danni was clutching her walking stick.

"Congratulations on 5 years!" Michael said to Mal and Leo.

"Thanks Michael. It's good to have you here." Leo replied.

"Yeah, I would've brought my date, but it seemed a little early." Michael admitted.

"How is that going?" Mal asked.

"It's lovely! It's quite nice to have something stable and consistent." Michael capitulated.

"She's lovely! She helped me find fabric for my next costume." Jamie chimed in.

"That's great! What's the next costume?" Leo asked.

"It's the main lady from 'Lust at First Bite.' Polly and I are going to do a duo for a comedy bit at the next championship." Jamie explained.

"I can't wait," Mal encouraged, "Speaking of championships, I'm going to go see Reuben and Danni." Mal left Michael, Jamie and Leo to speak to Danni and Reuben.

"My two champions!" Mal greeted them.

"Danni is the real champion," Reuben insisted.

"I can't believe I won the Nationals." Danni exclaimed.

"I can! That performance was amazing." Mal assured her.

"We're using our prize money from all the championships to go on a nice holiday." Reuben told Mal.

"We haven't had one since my fibromyalgia kicked into high gear, so this is long overdue." Danni explained.

"You two deserve it." Mal told them.

"Congrats again on your anniversary." Danni said. Mal hugged her.

"You're a peach," she gushed.

Two hours later, the food had been depleted. Polly and Mara were now hanging out with Reuben, Leo and Danni. Ariana and Sean were hanging out with Mal whilst Michael and Jamie chatted off to the side.

"You two look so happy." Leo told Mara and Polly.

"Thanks," Polly said bashfully.

"How was your weekend with Polly's parents?" Reuben quizzed.

"Wonderful!" Mara smiled. "They're lovely. It was nice to meet someone's parents and not have to correct the pronouns every 10 minutes."

"That's great!" Danni exclaimed.

"I best go back to the husband, but I'll be back in a while!" Leo explained to the group. Mara, Polly, Reuben and Danni continued chatting to each other. Leo linked arms with Mal, who was still with Ariana and Sean.

"I was just saying to Mal that it was kind of you both to invite me to your vow renewal." Ariana said.

"Of course! We love having you around." Leo gushed.

"How're you getting on there Sean?" Mal asked Sean.

"I'm okay today," Sean admitted. "I finally got the therapy assessment appointment and I printed off the copy of my restraining order." An uncomfortable pause followed.

"She was going to come up one way or another," Sean said with a shrug "She keeps trying to contact me."

"Yeah I think everyone had to block her on everything," Leo said.

"She doesn't take rejection well, does she?" Mal suggested.

"At least she can't physically approach Sean without getting put in a cell again." Ariana told them. Sean sighed. He looked at Danni who was happily in conversation.

"Do you think Danni would talk to me about things?" he said quietly.

"Have you talked much?" Leo asked.

"Yeah, but it's awkward - especially after Alexia hacked my account."

"Maybe this is the best time to talk to her?" Mal advised.

"Are you up to it Sean?" Ariana asked him tenderly.

"I am," Sean mustered. "I just don't know if she is."

"Wait outside. I'll have a quick chat with her. If she's up to it she'll come to you. If not I'll come get you and we'll head home," Ariana proposed.

"Thanks, sis."

"Go!" Ariana ordered. Sean headed outside the Suite. Ariana faced Leo and Mal.

"He owes you a thousand drinks if this works." Leo pointed out.

"I think this falls under 'supportive sister' duties. I sadly can't charge for that," Ariana replied.

She headed to Danni and tapped on her shoulder. Danni faced her.

"Ariana! Hey! How are you?" Danni greeted her enthusiastically.

"I'm alright. Listen, can I talk to you in private?" Ariana asked politely.

"Sure." Danni agreed. She handed her drink to Reuben, then she and Ariana moved away from everyone else.

"Sean is waiting outside the suite. He wants to talk to you," Ariana explained.

"Okay."

"You don't owe him a thing. What he did all those months ago was wrong. I'm only suggesting this to help you to clear the air and move forward one way or another." Ariana elaborated.

Danni sighed. She bit her lip.

Sean was waiting by the entrance of the Pavilion Suite, pacing back and forth. He was incredibly nervous.

"This is a really stupid idea," He complained out loud. "She's never going to come."

"Think again."

Sean turned to see Danni standing in the doorway.

"Danni. You came," He said, shocked.

"I know, right?" Danni responded. The atmosphere was intensely awkward but a romantic tension between the pair was clear.

"I shouldn't have slept with you when I did," Sean started. "It's not because I didn't want to, because I really did. But I dragged you into a toxic situation you didn't deserve to be forced into. You got hurt because of me. I'm really sorry." Danni looked down at the floor, unsure how to react.

"I still have feelings for you." Sean admitted. Danni looked back up at him.

"What?" She sputtered.

"I never stopped having feelings for you," Sean elaborated. "It killed me seeing you perform so beautifully and not being able to cheer you on. You're the most incredible woman I've ever met. These past months my feelings haven't changed." Danni could not believe what she was hearing.

"I don't know what to say to that." she stammered.

"I think we could be really great together. I have to earn your trust and I know that won't happen overnight. I would love to be one of your partners, but I understand if you can't trust me now." Sean continued. They looked intently at each other; a tension palpable between them.

"I think I need some time to think about this. If anything happens between us, we have to go slowly. Is that okay?" Danni replied. Sean smiled.

"Of course," Sean agreed. "I'll give you space." He started to head back into the Suite, but Danni stopped him. She kissed him passionately.

"A second was enough time, right?" Danni joked.

"If you like," Sean smiled at her.

ACKNOWLEDGEMENTS

With thanks to Sergey Kochergan, Txteva, Alex, Tom, Michael Kettle, Lauren Lee Hirst, Scarlet, Dani Kelly, Jenny, Anastasia Catris, Nat & Devin, Kit Kitson, Jennie Lumsden, Julianne Edwards, Kit Alloway, Serena Stampfer, TJ Green, Phil, Alex, Joe, Fia P, Sana Khan, and Colin from the Kickstarter campaign.

Ingram Content Group UK Ltd.
Milton Keynes UK
UKHW022136090323
418309UK00014B/962

9 781739 985905